"We'll have to go to the register office tomorrow morning to make the arrangements."

"Noah, you're not listening to me. I have absolutely no intention of marrying you on Wednesday or—"

"Thursday might be better," Noah agreed.

"Or any other day," Lizzie insisted.

"I've got an appointment first thing, but after that I'm free until the evening," he continued, disregarding her objection.

"I *am* busy on Thursday."

"You see, the great thing about having the ceremony on Thursday, Elizabeth, is that Francesca and Peter will be back from Stratford. We can… No, *you* can invite them to be our witnesses. What could be more perfect?"

He was serious. He really meant it….

Liz Fielding was born in Berkshire, England, and educated at a convent school in Maidenhead. At twenty she took off for Africa to work as a secretary in Lusaka, where she met her civil-engineer husband, John. They spent the following ten years working in Africa and the Middle East. She began writing during the long evenings when her husband was working away on contract. Liz and her husband are now settled in Wales with their children, Amy and William.

Conflict of Hearts
Liz Fielding

Harlequin Books

TORONTO • NEW YORK • LONDON
AMSTERDAM • PARIS • SYDNEY • HAMBURG
STOCKHOLM • ATHENS • TOKYO • MILAN
MADRID • WARSAW • BUDAPEST • AUCKLAND

ISBN 0-373-17320-2

CONFLICT OF HEARTS

First North American Publication 1997.

CHAPTER ONE

LIZZIE FRENCH jumped involuntarily as the church door clanged noisily behind a latecomer. Had he come? She had almost given up hope, but now, heart-in-mouth, she turned.

Too late. Whoever had entered the church had slipped into one of the pews at the back and was already hidden from sight.

'It was a middle-aged lady in a puce hat that perfectly matches her complexion.' Startled by this wickedly telling description of the vicar's wife, Lizzie involuntarily glanced at the man standing beside her.

Noah Jordan's dark brows were lifted just a fraction, his mouth turned down slightly at the corners in a mocking expression that might just have been an apology that he was the bearer of such disappointing news. But somehow she didn't think so.

She jerked her eyes back to the page in front of her, determined to shut the man out of her mind. But Noah Jordan refused to be shut out. Even as she stared at the order of service the grey sleeve of his morning coat brushed against the smooth golden skin of her shoulder while he turned the page for her, silently indicating the place with the tip of one long finger.

She could almost hear him laughing at her. And her father actually expected her to go and stay with the wretched man while he was away on his honeymoon... If only Peter would come!

She shifted, uncomfortably aware that she was being assessed by a pair of hawkish grey eyes that would miss nothing—certainly not the angry flush that coloured her cheeks. It was all too easy to imagine him examining a painting from a dubious source with just that look. The signature might be right, the provenance perfect, and yet...

Well, let him look. She didn't care one jot what he thought. Noah Jordan might have a reputation as a man with an infinite capacity to charm, but he hadn't charmed her. Not one bit.

Lizzie made a determined effort to concentrate on the service, and there were no more late arrivals to set her heart jangling. Only the unexpectedly disturbing touch of Noah's cool hand against her skin as he took her arm and they followed her father and his new bride into the vestry to sign the register.

'You don't much approve of this, do you?' Amidst the congratulations and kisses, Noah's words jolted her back to reality.

'I...' What could she say—Your sister is going to break my father's heart, and I know what that will do to him because I've been there before?

Her father hadn't believed her, so why should Noah Jordan? And so, for today, to make her father happy, she had smiled and played bridesmaid. But those probing, eagle-sharp eyes hadn't been fooled. Was that what puzzled him? Did he find it so impossible to believe that anyone would not welcome his dazzling sister as a stepmother?

Her eyes fell upon the laughing bride. She looked so happy, so radiant, so totally in love. But then she was a supremely gifted actress. 'Does it matter?' Lizzie asked. She made no further effort to pretend. The man could apparently see straight through her.

'Not to me. To your father... to Olivia it might,' he drawled, his voice making her skin tingle as if he were rubbing velvet the wrong way. 'What do you object to particularly?'

She raised her chin a little. 'She's a lot younger than Dad,' she said. 'It seems an odd match.' But if she'd hoped to divert him with the kind of gossip she overheard in the village shop she was mistaken.

'A lot younger?' he repeated thoughtfully, but he was unimpressed by this argument. 'She's thirty-four, Elizabeth. Hardly a girl.' His mouth compressed into a thin line. 'She won't run off and leave him for a younger man, if that's what is on that devious little mind of yours.'

Elizabeth. How she hated that. No one but her mother had ever called her that, except when she was in deep trouble. But then she was—in the deepest trouble. 'My father is nearly fifty,' she responded frostily.

His eyes creased to betray his wry, exasperated amusement at this remark. 'Olivia told me that he was a little over forty-five. I wonder which James would agree with?'

Oh, she knew that. Her father was as susceptible to flattery as the next man. But he would still be forty-nine next birthday. And, having nailed her objection so firmly to the mast, she wasn't about to back down just because Noah Jordan thought it was ridiculous. Besides, it served as well as anything else to cover the anger. That was private. Not for public consumption.

Her public face had smiled and smiled, and no one had suspected her true feelings. Why should they? Olivia was such an accomplished actress; who would ever guess what she was really like? But somehow this man knew the smile that Lizzie had painted on was only a mask.

'The age difference is still—' she pressed on, then stopped abruptly at the derision that momentarily twisted his mouth.

'Too great?' He completed her objection with the faintest touch of ridicule in his voice. 'Perhaps you think your father should have settled for some comfortable widow-lady and be content with carpet slippers and cocoa at bedtime?'

Under his taunting eyes she felt the colour rise again to her cheeks. Her father was an attractive man and it had been five years since her mother's death; he deserved a second chance at happiness. She had been glad for him that Olivia was beautiful, desirable. It was no more than he deserved after all the unhappiness since his first wife had died. That wasn't the reason for the cold anger that sat like a lump of lead in her stomach. But she was saved from the necessity of answering by the cause of her misery.

'Noah, darling, what on earth have you said to Lizzie to make the child blush so?' Olivia chided, with a soft laugh as she turned on her new husband's arm.

'This is a wedding, Olivia,' he responded, with a smile that creased his cheeks—a smile that came all too readily for his beautiful sister. 'Making the bridesmaid blush is all part of the fun.'

'Is it, indeed?' Olivia reached up and tapped his cheek warningly. 'Well, my dear, just make sure that's the only tradition involving bridesmaids and fun that you keep alive on this occasion.'

'Don't worry,' Lizzie breathed, with feeling, as Olivia turned away.

'She has no need.' Noah Jordan's voice was as low as hers. 'My duty was done when I gave away the bride. It's the best man's responsibility to see that the bridesmaid . . . has fun.'

The hateful blush deepened, but Noah was regarding the portly figure of her father's business manager, who had been conscripted to this duty. And for once genuine amusement unexpectedly lit the depths of those probing eyes as he considered what fun was likely to be had in that direction.

This totally unexpected betrayal of a sense of humour somehow irritated Lizzie even more than his attitude to her. 'I compliment you on your hearing, Mr Jordan,' she snapped.

'All my senses are in perfect working order, Elizabeth,' he replied gravely. 'Including the most important.'

'Which is?' she enquired, a little archly, then sincerely wished she hadn't as his brow rose a fraction higher.

The pause before he replied was infinitesimally brief. Yet it was there. 'Common sense, of course,' he said abruptly. 'And, since people will think it a little odd if you continue to refer to me as "Mr Jordan", you'd better get used to calling me Noah.'

'Maybe I would, if you'd stop calling me *Elizabeth* in quite that tone of voice.'

'And what "tone of voice" is that?' he asked softly.

Disapproving. As if she had been summoned by the headmistress for breaking a window. But he didn't need to be told. He knew exactly what tone of voice he was using. He reserved it especially for her.

But the organ had struck up. 'We'll resume this discussion on the drive to London, shall we?' Noah said, and, before she could tell him exactly what he could do with his drive to London, he had taken a firm grip on her arm and was leading her back down the aisle behind the bride and groom.

Toasts had been drunk and speeches made, and the guests were helping themselves from the buffet laid out in the marquee. But Lizzie wasn't hungry, despite the long hours that had elapsed since breakfast. Peter had not come, and all she wanted was the opportunity to escape the almost unbearable *bonhomie*. Her unhappiness was private. It had no place at a wedding. She lowered herself onto her favourite seat, half-hidden in an arbour that overlooked the rose garden.

'Lizzie...' She heard Olivia's voice calling from a little way off and stayed very still, hoping to remain unnoticed. But the voice came nearer, and she dashed a tear from her cheek and stood up to reveal herself rather than submit to the ignominy of being found hiding. 'Lizzie, my dear, there you are. I've been looking everywhere for you. I wanted to have a word...just the two of us before—'

'Are you going now?' Lizzie asked, a little stiffly.

Olivia's brow wrinkled slightly at the chill in her voice. 'No, darling.' Lizzie almost winced at the theatricality of the endearment. It would be so easy to be fooled, especially when you wanted to be, and for a while she had been... 'You'd better come and sit down, darling. There's something I have to tell you. Perhaps you've guessed...' Lizzie made no reply. 'James should have done it,' she pressed on. 'He's really been very naughty...'

Naughty! Lizzie thought she might just throw up. But whatever it was that Olivia wanted to say would have to wait as, beyond the fragile beauty of the bride, Lizzie at last saw her heart's desire.

'Peter!' Abandoning her new stepmother, she scooped up her long skirts and ran across the lawn towards the tall, slender figure of Peter Hallam. He stopped and turned as he heard her voice, and she flung herself into his arms. 'Oh, Peter!' And she was not sure whether to laugh or cry. 'You came. I knew you would.'

He didn't hold her close to him, but put her down and stood back, lifting his shoulder a little awkwardly. 'I was coming home anyway,' he said, looking around

anywhere not to meet her eyes. 'I can't wait to meet the
bride. I saw her in *Camille* last year. You must be very
happy, Lizzie.'

He was still angry with her. Hiding the hurt at this
cool reception, she told herself that a little reserve was
to be expected. Nevertheless, if he hadn't cared he
wouldn't have flown the Atlantic just to come to her
father's wedding. But her smile was a little hesitant as
she put her hand on his arm. 'It's good to see you, Peter.'

'Is it?'

He wanted her to grovel a little. A spark of re-
sentment took her by surprise, but she took a deep breath
and swallowed her pride. 'If the invitation to come to
New York is still open, I've got all the time in the world
now...'

She faltered as he stiffened. 'Lizzie...I've got something to tell you... It was all rather sudden...' Then
something like relief swept across his features. 'Fran!'
he called, and waved. 'We're over here.'

Lizzie watched, at first with confusion and then with
a growing sense of impending disaster, as a pretty dark-
haired young woman crossed the lawn towards them.

'Peter, honey, I've been looking for you. I don't know
a soul here, and your parents didn't exactly roll out the
red carpet—'

'Well, here's someone for you to meet,' he said quickly.
'I told you all about little Lizzie French, what a great
cook she is...' He attempted a light-hearted laugh.
'Perhaps you should ask her how she does it... Lizzie,
this is Francesca.' He took the girl's hand, and his mouth
tightened briefly before he added, 'My wife. I just know
you two are going to love one another.'

In the small, hollow silence that followed Fran extended a slender hand. 'You are *little* Lizzie?' she
queried. Five feet and nine inches tall, Lizzie hadn't been

'little' for a very long time, and she was a good three inches taller than the young woman before her.

'It's just a silly joke,' Peter said immediately. One that she and Peter had shared, as they had once shared everything. But shock had done something to her vocal cords, and her words were scarcely audible. His wife. The word echoed like the clang of doom. Wife... Wife... Wife...

'Have you known Peter long?' she managed, although her tongue was like a lump of wood in her mouth. Anything to stop that word...

'About six months. We work together at the bank.'

'Fran is an investment analyst,' Peter said. 'A graduate of Harvard Business School,' he added, as if it mattered.

'Oh.'

'What do you do, Lizzie?' Fran asked.

'Nothing much.' She wasn't prepared to compete.

'Lizzie keeps house for her father, Fran,' Peter interposed.

Fran glanced around, taking in the rambling red-brick house that had been extended through the centuries until it had become an impossible hotchpotch of styles—a nightmare to run, the bane and the love of Lizzie's life. 'Well, that must be a full-time job,' she said. 'Although I imagine your stepmother will take over now?'

Peter spoke before she could say something stupid, betray herself. 'Of course she will. Now that your father doesn't need you, Lizzie, you'll be able to leave home and get on with your life.' And Lizzie flinched at this jarring reminder that when Peter had needed her she had put her father first. But he didn't need her any more. Neither of them did. 'Perhaps you should get a job,' he advised, and she caught the harsh note of bitterness in the words.

'Like Fran?' she asked, still too shell-shocked to make her excuses and walk away.

'You wouldn't make much of an investment analyst, Lizzie,' he said. 'You never could weigh up the risks.' Did he have to rub in the fact that he believed she had made the wrong choice? How deeply she must have hurt him to make him so cruel. 'You're just too much of a home body, I guess.'

A *home body*! A flash of anger dulled the pain. He had never complained in the past. He had always enjoyed coming to the house, eating the food she cooked for him no matter what time of the day or night he arrived. 'Maybe you should look for something in catering,' he suggested, his memory clearly running along the same lines as hers.

'I'll certainly think about it.' Lizzie was smiling so hard that she thought her face must crack in half. But under the tense, searching eyes of his new wife she sought for something witty to say—a disguise for her broken heart. If only her head wasn't stuffed with cotton wool. Rescue came from an unexpected source.

'Elizabeth, I'm sorry to rush you, but we have to leave quite soon.' Noah's hand on her shoulder made her jump.

'Leave?' she repeated, still too dazed for anything to make much sense.

He didn't answer her. 'It's Hallam, isn't it? Noah Jordan. I've just been talking to your parents. I understand congratulations are in order.'

'Thank you,' he said, clearly relieved to break the tension. 'May I introduce my wife Francesca?'

Noah transferred his gaze to Peter's new wife and took her hand, holding it, it seemed to Lizzie, for ever. Then he seemed to recollect himself. 'I apologise for dragging Elizabeth away, but I'm taking her to see *Tosca* tonight—a treat for all the hard work she's put into organising the wedding for Olivia.' He glanced at Lizzie.

His heavy-lidded eyes gave no hint of his intention, but there was something about the determined cut of his mouth that suggested she would be wise to follow his lead.

'*Tosca*?' Fran repeated. 'That is absolutely my favourite opera,' she declared, obviously relieved to have a topic of conversation that had nothing to do with the unknown politics of a small village. 'I have a recording of my mother singing—'

'Your mother is a singer?' Lizzie felt Noah's long fingers tighten against her shoulder as he asked the question.

'Was. Not professional, of course, although she was very good. I have a recording of her singing and my father playing the piano.' She gave an awkward little smile. 'It's about all I have of them. They died when I was very young.'

Noah's eyes were fastened on the girl's face. 'Then you must come with us tonight.'

'We couldn't possibly...' Peter began, staring at Lizzie, his brows tugged together in a bewildered frown.

'I have a box with two empty seats. It would be a pity to waste them.'

'Oh, Peter, please!' Fran begged. 'Mr Jordan wouldn't have asked if he didn't mean it.' She turned eagerly back to Noah. 'Would you?'

Noah offered a reassuring smile. 'We'd love to have you as our guests.' He turned to Lizzie. 'Wouldn't we, darling?'

Darling? She was beginning to seriously hate that word. But before she could react he had slipped his arm about her waist. 'Seven o'clock at the Coliseum. If we miss you in the foyer, I'll leave a pass at the box office.' He raised a hand, and before Lizzie knew what was happening she was being propelled across the lawn towards the house.

'Lizzie...?' Peter's slightly puzzled voice trailed after her.

'Don't look back,' Noah rapped out, quite unnecessarily. Lizzie had no desire to look back. The picture of Peter standing confused and unhappy beside his bride would haunt her for ever. The dreadful suspicion that he had married Francesca on the rebound simply to spite her... She half stumbled across the grass in her haste to get as far away from them as possible.

As they reached the French windows that led to the drawing room, Noah turned her to him. Tears were turning his image into a watery blur as his fingers touched her chin and raised it a fraction, exposing her to the full force of a pair of seeking grey eyes. And while she stood there, held like a rabbit helpless in a pair of headlamps, he bent and kissed her.

His lips were cool and firm and dry against hers, and she caught the faintest scent of something indefinable that seemed to be the very essence of Noah Jordan. Shock held her rooted to the spot. Peter had kissed her many times, tenderly, warmly. But Noah Jordan's mouth was totally demanding, provoking a flicker of some undreamt-of desire...

She clutched at his wide shoulders as her head was forced back over his arm, shutting her eyes tightly in a desperate attempt to blot out what was happening, the realisation that it would be all too easy to respond. That she wanted to... But then it was over, his hand at her back as he swept her into the drawing room.

'What on earth do you think you're doing?' she demanded, turning on him angrily in her confusion. 'How dare you kiss me like that?'

'It's something people do at weddings,' he said carelessly. 'Kiss the bridesmaid. Or hadn't you noticed?'

She brushed aside his reference to the chaste salutes of family friends. 'It wasn't...the same.'

'No?' His expression was disquieting. 'Perhaps not. I promise not to let it go to my head.'

'You...' She tugged at her arm. 'Oh...let me go,' she stormed. 'I want—'

He swung her back into his arms, forcing her to face him, meeting her angry expression head-on. 'Everyone within a hundred yards could see what you wanted, Elizabeth. Including his wife. That's why I kissed you—to save the face of a young woman who has been pitchforked by that young fool into a very awkward situation. You've made the start of one marriage difficult enough. I don't intend to let you upset another. So you'd better go and change. Right now.'

So, she was right. Olivia had run to her brother and arranged this little plan to get her out of the way. It certainly explained his undisguised hostility. Well, she wasn't about to fall into line and co-operate with her eviction from her own home. 'Change?' she demanded. 'Why on earth would I want to change?'

'Because I have no intention of driving to London with you dressed like that. I'll come and pick up your bags in a few minutes. You'll need something long for tonight, by the way. It's a gala.'

She stood her ground. 'Don't be ridiculous, Mr Jordan. You're not driving me to London, or anywhere else for that matter. And I loathe the opera,' she added, without the slightest qualm at uttering such fiction.

'Noah,' he insisted, ignoring her protest. 'My sister has married your father. We're practically related. That's why I have been lumbered with you.'

'Rubbish,' she said. 'And you can consider yourself unlumbered. I'm perfectly happy here.'

One dark brow kinked at the vehemence of her reply, then his hands grasped her shoulders and forcibly propelled her towards the hall. 'Causing as much mischief as you can, no doubt. Think again. Staying here is not an option.' The hard edge to his voice left no room for doubt.

'But...' It was ridiculous. When her father had first broached the idea that she should stay with Noah for a few weeks after the wedding she hadn't made a fuss. She had made other plans—to visit New York with Peter...

She gave a little gasp as she was jolted back to reality. Her plans had been nothing but daydreams. But she still had a month while Olivia and her father were away to make her own arrangements. 'The house shouldn't be left empty,' she objected.

'I may have misread the situation, but I don't think you were planning on house-sitting for the next month, Elizabeth.'

She flushed angrily. 'My plans are none of your business.'

'I wish that were true,' he replied, with feeling. 'However, if you'd had the good manners to stay and listen to Olivia, instead of making a fool of yourself over Hallam, you would know that there's been a last-minute change of plan. She has been advised not to fly. Which is why, like it or not, you're coming to London with me. Right now.'

'Not to fly? Why on earth...?' Lizzie felt the angry flush drain from her cheeks. There could be only one reason why a perfectly fit woman shouldn't fly. 'She's pregnant!'

Noah eyed her sudden pallor. 'You didn't know?'

'Obviously not. Presumably, after all the lectures about the dangers of unwanted pregnancies, Dad found it difficult to tell me.'

A small muscle tightened at the side of his mouth. 'This baby may not have been planned, but if you believe that it's unwanted I suggest you think again. When I had lunch with your father last week he was overjoyed at the possibility of a son. I certainly understand why he wouldn't want any more daughters.' He glanced around him. 'Although I can see that you might be a little piqued at having to step aside and surrender all this for such a late arrival.'

'Step aside?' Lizzie repeated, too bewildered for a moment to respond more vigorously to his barely cloaked aggression. A baby? For a moment—just a moment—she thought that everything might, after all, work out. Then she knew, understood the full horror of that triumphant telephone call the day after the wedding had been announced, when Olivia had thought that she was in the house alone.

'We're saved, darling. I've got the man in the palm of my hand. Lord, but it took some acting to convince the old fool... But it's the perfect cover...'

There had been a pause and Olivia had laughed softly. 'I can't run away from my honeymoon, my darling, much as I'd like to. But after that, well... I'm keeping my London flat so I can see you any time I want. The only fly in the ointment is Daddy's little girl... she's so protective... but I'm working on a little plan to deal with her...' And after a few more seconds there had been the little ting as the phone had been replaced.

And Olivia hadn't wasted any time putting her plan into action. The next day her father had called her into the study and suggested that she might like to spend a few weeks in London. It would give Olivia a chance to take control of the house, he had explained. With Lizzie there...well, the staff would naturally look first to her... He knew she would understand.

Olivia's brother had kindly offered to put Lizzie up at his London home for a few weeks, he told her. There had been just a touch of awkwardness about his smile. She had spent too much time looking after her old dad, he'd said, and patted her hand. Noah would see that she had some real fun.

How reasonable it would have sounded if she hadn't known better. It was then that she had made the mistake of trying to tell her father what Olivia was really like beneath that sugar-sweet exterior.

Now she stared at Noah. Whatever 'little plan' Olivia had devised, her brother was quite obviously a part of it. 'Excuse me,' she said, turning abruptly away.

'Quick as you can, Elizabeth. And don't forget the long dress.'

She glared at him, but didn't bother to reply. She would be quick, but not because he demanded it. Her own desperate need to get away from all of them was encouragement enough. And she certainly wouldn't be needing a long dress.

She regarded her reflection in the cheval-glass in the corner of her bedroom with distaste. Was it only a few hours ago when she had stood in that same spot, certain that if Peter responded to her olive branch, came to the wedding, it might just be possible to make a life for herself, to be strong for the time when her father would need her again?

She stripped off the cream silk dress and threw it on the bed, then tore the tiny rosebuds from her hair, angrily brushing it until she had obliterated every vestige of the hairdresser's art and it hung as straight and plain as a yard of tap water down her back. Then she felt marginally better, back in control, because if they all thought that she was going to fall in with the plans Olivia had made to dispose of 'Daddy's little girl' they could think again.

She would spend a few nights with an old school-friend who lived on the outskirts of London. It would give her time to sort herself out and make some decisions about the future. She certainly wasn't going anywhere with Noah Jordan. Not even, she thought, with just the tiniest regret, to the opera.

Then she took a deep breath and, dressed in her most comfortable jeans and a defiant scarlet T-shirt, she descended to the hall.

Noah was waiting at the foot of the stairs. He took in her change of appearance with a single, exasperated glance, and for just a moment she felt a touch of something between anger and shame. She'd wanted to shout her rage to the world. Too late she realised that flaunting her pain was simply emphasising her humiliation.

But there was no time for self-analysis because he seized her arm and thrust her back up the stairs before she could utter more than the feeblest protest. He didn't bother to ask which room was hers. He simply flung open every door he passed until he came to the one where her silk dress had slipped and crumpled into an untidy heap on the rosebud-strewn carpet, betraying her misery.

He stepped over it without comment, flung open her wardrobe and began to flip through the remaining contents.

'What on earth do you think you're doing?' she demanded as she regained the use of her tongue, furiously pushing herself between him and her clothes.

'I'm not about to walk out of here with you in a pair of jeans—'

'Mr Jordan, you're not about to walk out of here with me, full stop!'

He ignored this outburst and reached over her head to lift a soft voile print dress from its hanger. 'Put this on.' He turned back to the wardrobe. 'Is this the only evening dress you have?'

She regarded the pink taffeta garment with loathing. 'That's none of your business.'

He flipped it across his arm without comment and glanced around. 'Where are your bags?'

'Downstairs. In the boot room,' she said, crossing her fingers, fairly sure that he wouldn't know where that was.

He glanced at his watch. 'Very well. I'll see you downstairs in three minutes.'

'And if I refuse to change?' she flung at his retreating back.

He turned in the doorway and regarded her with a slow look that travelled from the toes of her hard-worn trainers to the top of her defiant head, and quite unexpectedly her lips began to burn with the memory of that fierce kiss. Her hand flew to cover her mouth, as if somehow he might be able to tell. He followed the movement and his eyes snapped ominously. 'I'll change you myself,' he said abruptly. 'Anything else?'

'I...' She tried to speak, but the word came out as little more than a hoarse croak. She cleared her throat, but he wasn't interested.

'No? Two and a half minutes.' Then he was gone.

And she made it, adding a dashing straw hat for good measure, and drawing on a pair of white lace gloves as she raced to the head of the stairs. Having decided to change, there was no point in being half-hearted about it. Then, as he heard her and turned, she slowed and sauntered down as if she had had all the time in the world. Noah's face was in shadow, so even if she cared she could not have seen his expression.

'Now we'll go and say goodbye to Olivia and James,' he said firmly.

'I'm sure they won't notice one way or the other,' she said, unable to keep the bitterness from her voice.

'Would you have it any other way?' It was a rebuke, and it brought hot little patches of colour to Lizzie's cheeks. 'But then, if Peter Hallam had flung himself into your willing arms instead of spoiling the perfect scenario by arriving with his brand-new wife, you wouldn't have been noticing much either, would you?'

'How can you be so beastly?'

'It takes years of practice,' he assured her.

'Don't be so modest, Mr Jordan,' she said fervently. 'You clearly have a natural talent for it.'

His brows rose a fraction. 'Careful, Miss Sweetness. Your claws are showing.'

'Miss Sweetness'? What was that supposed to mean? She clenched her teeth, determined not to rise to such an obvious attempt to bait her. Why on earth did the man have to be so unpleasant? Even if Olivia had told him that she had tried to interfere with the wedding plans, surely he must know what his sister was like? It wasn't *her* fault, so why was she attracting such venom from the man?

But he was right about one thing. Despite the fact that her father had barely spoken to her since her attempt to open his eyes, she wouldn't make things worse between them. None of this was his fault. And he had misery enough in store.

So she took a deep breath and braced herself, knowing that there must be pitying speculation about her feelings since Peter's arrival with his new bride. Every head would turn as she made her way across the lawn. So she had better be smiling. Noah took her arm and tucked it into his, holding it there when she would have pulled away.

'Forget any plans you have to make a scene, Elizabeth, or, I promise you, I will put you over my knee and spank you.'

Startled, she turned to stare at him. What did he think she was going to do—fling herself down on the grass and drum her heels like a spoilt child who'd lost her dolly? 'I'd just like to get this over with,' she said. 'As quickly as possible.'

But Noah refused to be hurried. Despite his insistence that they were short of time, he stopped to shake hands and say goodbye to a number of new acquaintances, and she was able to witness at first hand his undoubted charisma. By the time he delivered her to her father she was certainly the object of considerable speculation. But pity had nothing to do with it.

How was it, everyone clearly wanted to know, that little Lizzie French was leaving the wedding on the arm of the one man that every other woman would have given her eye-teeth to be with?

CHAPTER TWO

JAMES FRENCH turned as his daughter approached. 'Lizzie, there you are. Are you leaving now?' he said, a little awkwardly.

She wanted to fling her arms about his neck and hug him—longed to be able to tell him how happy she was for him, but the lie would stick in her throat. Lord, how she wished that she hadn't overheard that conversation.

'Noah has explained about the honeymoon having to be cancelled,' she said stiffly, turning quickly as she saw the painful reproach in his eyes. 'If you'd told me sooner, Olivia, I could have arranged...' She lifted her shoulders in a tiny shrug. 'But there's plenty of food in the freezer. You won't starve.'

'Olivia has arranged a hamper...' James French took hold of his new wife's hand and squeezed it reassuringly. 'She's been quite amazing.'

'Amazing,' Lizzie agreed dully. She had helped, encouraged, supported her father for the better part of five difficult years, until the long black tunnel of depression he had been living in had begun to open out and he had been able to begin to work again, to live again. But Olivia had picked up the telephone and ordered a hamper from Fortnum's and she was 'amazing'. Well, Olivia would soon discover that life at Dove Court was not the bed of roses that she had obviously imagined.

The object of her speculation was talking quietly to Noah. 'I know it's a lot to ask.'

'It's no trouble. Just forget about everything but yourself and James.' Noah caught Lizzie's blue eyes re-

24

garding him sceptically and he straightened. 'Shall we go?' he said abruptly.

'If you're quite ready,' she murmured, and reluctantly submitted to the hollow ritual of cheek-kissing.

'Lizzie...' Olivia hesitated for just a moment under her expressionless eyes, then shook her head. 'Nothing. Just...enjoy yourself,' she urged. 'You haven't had much fun...'

'Fun'. The word rang tauntingly in her ears as they made their way back to the house.

'Noah...' Olivia had followed them, and her summons made him pause and turn.

'Get in the car, Elizabeth. I'll be with you in a minute.'

She made her way towards the vintage drophead Bentley, gleaming silver, its top down in the glorious summer sunshine. Her pink dress lay on the back seat along with Noah's top hat. He was welcome to it.

She kept walking until she was in the cooler shade of the garage. Her car was at the far end and she climbed in, fitted the key and turned it. The engine obediently whirred, but did not catch. She tried again. Shock was beginning to overtake her. She was trembling, and her fingers slipped on the key as she tried for the third time to start the car.

The door beside her opened and she leaned back in the driving seat, admitting defeat. 'What have you done?' she asked.

'Anticipated your every move.' Noah leaned against the roof of her Metro and held out a small metal object for her inspection. 'It's called a rotor arm. I'm afraid you car won't start without it.'

She stared uncomprehendingly for a moment. 'How did you know?'

'You lied about the luggage. Since you were planning to leave, this was the obvious place to look. I've already moved it to my car.' He stood back, his face expressionless. 'Shall we go?'

'I'm not going anywhere with you,' she protested. 'I'm going to stay with a friend in Islington for a few days until I sort myself out. And I'm perfectly capable of driving myself.'

'Nonsense,' he snapped. 'You're in no condition to drive anywhere.'

'I'm just fine.'

'Really?' He grasped her wrist and held her hand in front of her eyes. 'You're shaking, Elizabeth. And how many glasses of champagne did you drink?'

'I wasn't counting,' she snapped back.

'There was no need to. I don't imagine you were planning to drive yourself down the M40 into London on this Saturday evening. You were going to let Peter Hallam do that.'

Damn the man! Why did he have to be right about everything? She took a deep breath. 'You can give me a lift,' she compromised.

'How generous of you.' And, with an ironic little twist to his mouth, he straightened and opened the door wide for her. She slipped out of her seat and fled across the yard to his car, not waiting for him to open the door.

'Ready?' he asked as he climbed in beside her. She took a last long look at the garden and the people standing about in small knots—friends, relations, people she had known all her life. Then she saw Peter. As if he could feel her eyes upon him, he turned and stared at her. Then Fran followed his glance and she also stared at Lizzie, her brow drawn down in a small frown. Noah had seen it too.

'Fasten your seatbelt, Elizabeth,' he said abruptly. She did so, then sank back against the old leather and closed her eyes. 'And take off your hat, or you'll lose it. There's a scarf in the glove box.'

Would she never have a moment of peace to shed a tear for what she had thrown away? Apparently not. When she made no immediate move to obey he leaned across and removed her hat for her, flipping it onto the rear seat to keep his top hat company. Then he opened the glove compartment and thrust a long silk chiffon scarf at her.

'Here.' She continued to stare fiercely at her gloves, unwilling to betray her weakness, but he caught her chin and turned her face towards him. She blinked furiously, but too late.

For a moment he stared as the tears welled onto her cheeks, then with an impatient gesture he wiped them from her face with the pads of his thumbs. And he wrapped the scarf around her hair in a movement so practised that she was certain he had done it a hundred times before, holding her against his chest as he tied it at the nape of her neck. 'Just how old are you, Elizabeth?' he asked.

'Twenty-one.' Her voice was muffled against the lapel of his morning coat, her ear only hearing the steady thump of his heart.

'As old as that?' The doubt in his voice touched off a dangerous spark of anger, driving her away from the deceptive comfort of his broad shoulder. She fought down an intense desire to slap the man, but only because she knew without a shadow of a doubt that he would slap her back. 'Far too old to be mooning over a calf-love. Did you actually believe him when he said he would marry you?' She stared at him. 'Surely your mother told you that a young man in the grip of his libido will promise anything to get his way?'

Dark colour seared her cheek-bones. 'Doubtless you speak from experience.'

'No, Elizabeth. I'm old enough to take care not to make promises I have no intention of keeping.'

'I can imagine. Although your status as a confirmed bachelor is so public I can't imagine that expectations on that score can be very high.'

'I have never failed to make my position clear.'

'That's all right, then.'

'It saves complications.'

'What about love? Doesn't that complicate things?' she demanded.

'Love?' He turned away, switched on the ignition, pressed the starter and the car purred into life. 'I learned a long time ago to distrust the word. Much safer to treat the whole idea as a spectator sport—on a par with bungee-jumping or free-fall parachuting.'

'Didn't I read somewhere that you once were a member of the Dangerous Sports Club?'

'Did you?' He shrugged. 'I didn't say I never participated, Elizabeth, only that I knew the risks involved.' His lips tightened in a horrible parody of his smile as she drew in a sharp breath. 'Have I shocked you? Well, you're very young. Still naïve enough to believe in such rubbish. You'll learn.'

'Just how old do you have to be before you get that cynical?' she asked.

'Not very old,' he said, with feeling, and she thought for the most fleeting moment that she had managed to dent his insufferable arrogance. But then the blade-edged smile was firmly back in place. 'I'm not quite in my dotage, but by your own demanding standards, Elizabeth, I'm far too old for you,' he replied very firmly. 'I can assure you that whatever you may hear to the contrary you will be perfectly safe under my roof. I wouldn't touch you with a bargepole.'

'You...' She barely managed to stop herself from telling him in the most graphic terms what he could do with his bargepole. 'You kissed me,' she pointed out, and achieved a certain sharp satisfaction in contradicting him.

'And I shall do so again if the situation requires it,' he replied, unmoved. 'But we'll both know that it doesn't mean a thing.'

The slow burn of anger helped, she found. While she kept her mind simmering on the obnoxious Noah Jordan she could almost forget about Peter.

'You kiss very... thoroughly...' she said, deliberately provoking him. 'I'm sure I shall learn a lot.'

'And you kiss like a virgin.'

She pressed her tongue hard against her teeth to stop herself from screaming at him that there was a very good reason for that.

'Kissed once when I wasn't looking,' she misquoted a little shakily, 'and never kissed again, even though I was looking all the time?'

'No doubt you'll improve with practice.' For a moment she thought that she detected that errant touch of humour in his voice. But his face, when she turned, was stony.

'Don't bother to apply for the position of coach. It isn't vacant.'

'On the contrary.' Her blush deepened painfully under his searching glance, but she refused to be intimidated. 'However, tonight I think we must do our best to convince the new Mrs Hallam that it has already been filled.' He slowed as they reached the main road, and for a moment concentrated on the traffic. Once they were moving along smoothly again he continued. 'After that you can do whatever you like.'

'What would you suggest?' she prompted. Anything rather than dwell on the thought of Mrs Hallam, she thought.

His eyes lingered on her for a moment, then he turned away. 'I hardly think I'm the best person to advise you,' he said abruptly.

'You've been pretty free with your advice until now,' she declared.

He shrugged. 'I suggest you do whatever is necessary to take your mind off Peter Hallam. Isn't there something you've always wanted to do, but never had the chance?'

Another reminder that it was time to be moving on? 'So long as it isn't bungee-jumping or free-fall parachuting?' she offered sourly.

'You're young enough to survive a few painful landings.' Heartache wasn't fatal, then? She thought it was a little early to say. She was still numb with shock. But fighting with Noah Jordan was certainly a very effective diversion. He threw her a fleeting glance. 'Have you ever lived away from home? Actually worked for a living?'

He made her sound like a parasite. 'No. But it looks as if I'm about to get my first taste of both. I don't have much choice, do I? I've been given my marching orders.'

'Marching orders?' His surprise was very convincing, but she wasn't fooled.

'Frankly, Noah, I don't understand why you're taking so much interest.'

His mouth thinned. 'Like you, Elizabeth, I had my arm twisted.'

'Well, you can consider it untwisted. Just take me to Islington.' He didn't bother to reply, and for a while they travelled in silence. Then Lizzie glanced at the man beside her. 'Was I really so transparent? Back there?' she was finally driven to ask.

He threw her a cursory look. 'As the Crystal Palace with all the lights on.' She paled. 'I assumed you wanted an honest answer.'

'There's honest,' she replied stiffly, 'and there's brutal.' She stared straight ahead. 'I'll never be able to look that girl in the face again.'

'You're going to have to. I invited them to join us tonight.'

'They won't miss me.'

'On the contrary, your absence would be impossible to attribute to anything other than... pique.'

'Pique?'

'Jealousy is such a nasty word.'

Lizzie frowned. Jealous? She had always imagined jealousy to be a sour, hateful emotion. This hollow, empty feeling had none of that. But there was no time to consider the matter as Noah claimed her attention.

'You will be charming to Francesca, you will behave towards Peter like the doting little sister he has doubtless portrayed you as to his wife, and you will treat me...' He said nothing for a moment, but as they slowed and came to a halt for the motorway roundabout he raised heavy lids to run an assessing glance over her. It was unnerving.

Something in that look—the slightest darkening of a pair of steely eyes—brought a fierce glow to her cheeks and played havoc with her pulse, sending it crashing into overdrive. Whatever he wanted from her, she didn't think she was going to like it.

A blast on a car horn behind them made her jump. Noah raised an apologetic hand and turned his attention back to the road.

'What?' Lizzie demanded.

'You will treat me as if we are lovers,' he said with absolute conviction.

Lizzie swallowed, hard. She'd been right. She didn't like it one bit. 'And how am I supposed to do that from the end of a bargepole?'

'You can safely leave all the details to me.' If Noah had meant to be reassuring he failed signally. His kiss still burned like a brand on her lips, and the suggestion that there was more to come sent a tremor of apprehension rippling through her midriff. 'So?' he asked once he had negotiated the slip-road. 'What do you plan to do with yourself in London?'

'I haven't had much time to make plans,' she said.

'But surely you...?' Then he went on, 'No, of course you wouldn't have made any plans for London. You were planning on a trip to New York with young Mr Hallam.' His chiselled features were rock-hard. 'Well, Olivia asked me to make sure you had some fun.' He made it sound like hard labour. 'I'm sure I'll think of something. I'll have to. It's clear that you've never had to stand on your own two feet.'

Her denial was whipped away by the wind as he put his foot down and the Bentley cruised majestically past a row of lorries. It couldn't matter less, Lizzie thought, but he was so wrong about her. She had stood very firmly on her own two feet ever since her mother had died. And she had been a very firm prop for her father too.

'That really won't be necessary, Noah. I shall be staying with my friend until I find somewhere to live. And I'm quite capable of keeping myself occupied.'

At least money wouldn't be a problem. She had hardly touched the allowance that her father had given her since she had taken over the running of the house, and her mother had left her some money. A dowry, she had called it. Well, she wouldn't be needing a dowry now. But she needed somewhere to live as a matter of urgency.

It was impossible to conduct a conversation in an open car travelling at high speed, but even when they reached the end of the motorway and slowed for London traffic Noah seemed disinclined to resume their conversation, deep in his own brooding thoughts. Finally she was driven to break the silence.

'Islington was that way,' she pointed out as they passed a road sign.

'If I ever need a navigator I'll bear you in mind. But we're not going to Islington.'

'You may not be... I certainly am.' He ignored her. 'You disabled my car so that I was forced to come with you,' she went on a little desperately. 'Now you must take me to my friend's flat, or drop me at the nearest underground station if you prefer. I can easily make my own way from there.'

'Must?' For a moment the word hung between them, then, with the slightest shrug, he let it go. 'It's a sunny Saturday evening in August, Elizabeth. Do you suppose your friend is sitting at home on the off chance that you might decide to descend upon her and demand a bed for the night?'

The thought had already crossed her own mind, but she had no intention of admitting it. She would rather stay at a hotel than accept this man's hospitality. 'She's always inviting me to come up for the weekend,' she protested.

'But, since she's not expecting you, you have to address the possibility that she may be out.'

'She'll come back.'

'This is London, Elizabeth, not some leafy country village. Sitting around on doorsteps surrounded by your baggage is not to be recommended. And I did promise your father...' He clearly wished he hadn't. 'Besides, you and I have a date with a lady called Tosca.'

'I told you—'

'You told me that you loathe the opera,' he interrupted a touch acerbically. 'The collection of records and CDs in your room is simply for decoration?'

She bitterly regretted her impetuous lie as it came back to haunt her. 'No,' she admitted.

'No,' he agreed, with an assurance that set her teeth on edge. 'I had planned to take you to see a show, but Olivia said you would much prefer the opera.'

Olivia. How clever of her. But she wasn't to be won over that easily. As Noah brought his car to a halt Lizzie looked up at the impressive terrace—anywhere rather than face those all-seeing eyes. The façade was as polished as the man. Even the tubs of brilliant flowers that flanked the doorway shone as if they had just been dusted. She distrusted such perfection. 'I would prefer it if you took me to my friend's flat,' she persisted stubbornly.

'Nonsense. One night in a crowded bedsit, sharing a bathroom with heaven knows how many other people, would drive you mad. You're simply not used to it. Besides, your invitation was for a weekend. What will you do then? If you think you can go creeping back to Daddy...'

Go back? She could never go back. She might be invited for the odd weekend, or Sunday lunch. But Dove Court would never be her home again. 'I intend to find a job, somewhere to live in London.'

'And how long do you imagine that will take? Or do you believe employers will be falling over themselves to offer you work?' he mocked.

'No, but...' But what? Still she didn't move, unwilling to put her main objection into words. She had seen the heads turn as they'd left the wedding. One or two raised eyebrows. And his kiss was still burned into her memory. And it was his stated intention to convince Peter that he was her lover. It might be ridiculous... It *was* ridiculous...

Noah had no such inhibitions. He lightly touched her cheek, turning her to face him. 'If I were in the market for a girl on the rebound, Elizabeth, I can assure you that I would have had you eating out of my hand by now.'

Her blue eyes widened and, ignoring the odd little tremor low in her stomach, which had been provoked by the touch of his hand against her skin, she managed a small laugh. 'You're remarkably confident of your attraction,' she said.

He regarded her solemnly. 'Don't you believe I could do it?'

And then he smiled. All the way up until little pouches creased beneath his eyes. Impossible to fake that. And his mouth was bracketed by strong, deep lines carved into his cheeks. She swallowed hard.

'Just what are you in the market for, Noah?' she asked, a little shakily, avoiding the need to give him a direct answer.

The smile abruptly disappeared, and he removed his hand from her chin. 'Nothing. My life is exactly the way I like it. Except for you.' He got out of the car and came round to open her door. Before she could respond the front door swung open and a middle-aged woman stood in the entrance.

Noah turned. 'And, as you see, you will be adequately chaperoned. Mrs Harper, this is Miss Elizabeth French,' he said, his hand in the small of her back propelling her up the steps to the front door. 'You'd better take her straight up to her room; we're going out at seven.'

'Of course, Mr Jordan. This way, Miss French.'

Lizzie hesitated. 'Noah, this is—'

'Mr Harper will bring your bags up in a moment,' he said, not allowing her to finish, his eyes daring her to defy him. She was trapped. At least for tonight. She would have to go through with his horrible plan. But tomorrow she would leave. Nothing would stop her.

'How did the wedding go?' Mrs Harper asked as she led the way up the stairs. 'Such a lovely day for it. I'm sure Miss Olivia must have looked quite beautiful. Your father is a lucky man.'

She chattered on, not waiting for answers to her questions. 'Now, these are your rooms. This is the sitting room. Your bedroom is through there, and your bathroom. I expect you'll want a shower after driving with the top down. Miss Olivia always says that she feels as if she's covered in "essence of motorway" after driving with Mr Jordan.' She chuckled. 'I'll go and fetch you a tray of tea.'

The woman's endless chatter was oddly comforting—normal in a world that had turned upside down. 'Thank you, Mrs Harper.'

The woman took the bags that her husband brought to the door and hung Lizzie's dress over the wardrobe door. 'Shall I unpack for you?'

'Oh, no. I can do that. Thank you,' Lizzie repeated a little belatedly as the woman withdrew.

She stared at the pale pink taffeta dress. It had been bought when she'd had to accompany her father to a formal dinner a couple of years earlier and had been worn only once. It was a little creased, but otherwise fine.

She pulled a face. No, it wasn't. It was awful. It had been her father's choice, and had been too young for her even then. But when she had protested he'd said that he wanted everyone to be sure she was his daughter, that he was not some foolish middle-aged man out with a bimbo. It had been hard enough to get him out of the house; she hadn't been about to argue over the dress. Well, it would have to do—it was all she had. She quickly stowed the remainder of her belongings and went to take her shower.

Ten minutes later she emerged from the bathroom to find a tray laid with a pot of tea and a plate of tiny sandwiches waiting for her. Her dress had disappeared.

As she sipped her tea she sat at the dressing table wondering what to do with her hair. It was ridiculously long, she decided, twisting it up into a simple chignon. If she left it loose, with the pink dress it would simply emphasise the 'Alice in Wonderland' look. There was a tap on the door.

'Come in,' she called. It was Mrs Harper with her dress. And another gown, black and elegant, on a padded satin hanger.

'I've pressed your dress, Miss French,' she said, 'but...' The woman was clearly embarrassed. 'Mr Jordan suggested you might...um...prefer to wear this.'

'Prefer'? She had the feeling that he had said something a great deal stronger than that. A closer look at her dress had doubtless warned him that she wouldn't look like anyone's lover in such a garment—certainly not that of the urbane, the very sophisticated Mr Jordan.

What would he consider suitable? she wondered, regarding the black dress with interest. It was an exquisite, ankle-length black shift in the finest silk jersey, with long, straight sleeves, a scooped-out neck and not a single

detail to distract from the purity of the line. It was simply
beautiful.

But then, the man was a world-renowned art dealer.
He had appeared in his own series on the television, discussing the merits of twentieth-century art, the unexpected success of which had been the devastating charm
of the presenter rather than the subject matter. His good
taste had never been in doubt.

'Thank you, Mrs Harper. It's...very kind of Mr
Jordan.'

The woman was clearly relieved at her reaction. 'It
should fit you well enough. Miss Olivia isn't quite as
slender as you, but that fabric clings rather, so I'm sure
you'll get away with it.'

'This is Olivia's dress?' She hadn't given a thought as
to where the gown might have come from. But Olivia
had been staying with Noah for the last few weeks while
her own apartment had been decorated. Something in
her voice must have betrayed her.

'It will look lovely on you, Miss French,' Mrs Harper
pressed, a little anxiously. 'I know Miss Olivia wouldn't
mind...'

Lizzie minded. She minded a great deal. But that
wasn't Mrs Harper's problem. 'Please call me Lizzie,'
she said, offering a reassuring smile. And Mrs Harper
smiled with relief and left.

She quickly made up her eyes and flicked blusher over
her cheek-bones, leaving her tan to take care of the rest.
Then, ignoring the black shift, she slipped into the pink
taffeta dress. It was a little tight across the bodice; she
had fulfilled the early promise of womanhood since she
had last worn it. She tugged up the zip and then, very
slowly, released her breath. It held, and for a moment
she regarded her reflection with a certain amount of
grim satisfaction.

Then she fastened a pair of pearl studs to her ears and touched the oval locket that she always wore about her throat before going down the broad staircase in search of her nemesis. She was now quite cheerfully prepared to convince the world that she was Noah's lover. But somehow she didn't think he would be quite so eager.

He was staring at a painting as she entered the drawing room, his thick dark hair a crisp counterpoint to the immaculate perfection of black broadcloth that emphasised his wide, square shoulders. For a moment she was struck by the sheer grace, almost beauty of the man. How easy it would be to fall under his spell, if he chose to cast it, she thought. Then he turned as he heard her move towards him.

The feeling was clearly not reciprocated. Regarding Lizzie in silence, Noah's glance moved quite deliberately in a chilling inspection of her appearance. She lifted her chin a little and stood her ground, although the fine hairs at the nape of her neck stirred as she sensed that her defiance had made him very angry indeed.

But as he moved towards her it wasn't her dress that claimed his attention. It was the locket.

He laid the tip of one finger against it, his eyes dark as thunderclouds as he fixed her to the spot. Then, without warning, he grasped it in his hand and jerked it from her throat, the old, delicate chain offering no resistance to this brutal treatment.

'No!' Lizzie's hand instinctively reached out to retrieve the precious object. But his hand snapped shut, and he dropped the locket into his pocket.

'What were you going to do, Elizabeth? Show Francesca your pretty antique locket? It's old and no doubt the clasp is worn, and if by chance it should happen to fall open...' He turned away in disgust. Lizzie swallowed.

'Please give it back to me.'

'I'll have it repaired,' he said abruptly.

'That doesn't matter. I just want it back.'

'You can have it when Mr and Mrs Hallam are safely back across the Atlantic.' He indicated the sideboard. 'Would you like a drink? I have a feeling that we're both going to need one to get through this evening.'

'You invited them. You have the drink.' She turned away, unable to bear to look at him, staring instead at the painting that had claimed his attention—a very traditional portrait of a young woman. Oddly out of place amongst Noah's collection of modern art, the sitter looked vaguely familiar... She took a step towards it.

'Sherry? Gin and tonic?' he persisted.

She didn't drink very much, but her throat was dry. 'A tonic water,' she conceded.

She heard the chink of ice, the fizz of tonic, then he walked across the magnificent Aubusson carpet until he was standing beside her. 'Elizabeth?'

'Thank you,' she said, turning to take the crystal tumbler from his hand.

'You're entirely welcome.' And he poured the contents of the glass down the demure *décolletage* of her gown.

CHAPTER THREE

LIZZIE caught her breath in a long, shuddering gasp as the icy liquid ran inside her dress, inside her bra, darkening the delicate fabric as it spread coldly to her waist.

For a moment Noah regarded his handiwork impassively. Then his eyes rose to meet hers. 'You appear to have a piece of...' He paused and fished a slice of lemon from the neckline of her dress. It was the last straw.

She swung at him and caught his cheek as he rocked back on his heels. She was certain that she had barely made contact, and yet the mark of her hand was there, livid against his sun-darkened skin.

He moved swiftly to capture her wrist, holding it fast in his strong fingers. 'Once, Elizabeth. Just once,' he warned. 'Try that again and I promise you won't sit down for a week.' For a moment she fought him, her cheeks hectic, her breath coming in furious gasps. Then, with a long tremulous sigh, she subsided.

'I'm sorry.'

'You're only sorry that you didn't hit me harder,' he said in a voice that struck like steel against her bones. Then he dropped her hand. 'Now go and change.' And this time she didn't bother to ask what he would do if she refused.

In the safety of her bedroom Lizzie came close to panic, stripping off her wet things, dropping them on the bathroom floor, desperate to change before Noah took it into his head to follow her and make certain she obeyed him.

41

The man was a monster. He had the ability to provoke the most outrageous feelings in her. She had never hit anyone in her life before—had never wanted to. But he had known only too well that she would have done it again, given the opportunity. She shivered, shaken by the intensity of her reaction to him.

'Oh, for goodness' sake, Lizzie. The wretch drowned you in ice. You're just cold,' she told herself crossly, sponging herself with warm water until she was rid of the sticky tonic water, and towelling herself dry. But she was still shivering.

Impatiently she tugged the black dress from its hanger and lifted it over her head, letting the material slide over her body until it came to rest against her hips. She glanced briefly at her reflection and then, startled, took a second look. The dress could have been made for her. The simple elegance, the purity of the line was so right.

Then she turned, and for the briefest of moments she was shocked at this very different vision of herself. As she moved the dress clung, offering a tantalising glimpse of her figure as she moved. It might be borrowed glamour, but Noah had been right to insist upon it. Lizzie had the feeling that tonight she was going to need all the help she could get.

She forced herself to say the painful words out loud. 'Francesca Hallam. Mrs Francesca Hallam.' Lord, how it hurt! But she had no one but herself to blame. Peter had warned her.

'Three times, Lizzie. I've asked you to marry me three times. Once I leave for New York, that's it.' The next day an envelope with an airline ticket had been delivered by courier from London. By Concorde to New York. One way. It had been an ultimatum and it had infuriated her. She had sent it back by return. Such stupid, stupid pride. If only she had tried a little harder to make him understand.

'Elizabeth?' There was a tap at her sitting room door, and it was something of a relief to drag her eyes away from the pale reflection in the mirror and dwell instead on the flare of anger that his voice alone was enough to provoke.

'What do you want?' The door opened and she glared at him. 'I didn't invite you in.'

'I'm not in the habit of conducting conversations through doors.' He regarded her changed appearance without comment. 'I would like you to wear these.'

The rejection of anything he offered was already half formed on her lips, but before she could speak he opened a flat jeweller's box to reveal a pendant and a pair of long, drop earrings that quite took her breath away.

'Oh!' She reached out a tentative finger to touch the stones. 'How... beautiful.'

'Yes, they are beautiful.' He took the pendant from its bed of velvet. It hung for a moment from his long fingers, the pearls glowing softly, the diamonds flashing fire in the dying sunlight. 'And will look very much better with that dress than your locket.'

This reminder of what he had done to her locket brought her back to earth with a jolt, and she stepped back. 'No.'

'I insist, Elizabeth.' His mouth was a thin, hard line. 'It will add to the illusion—'

'That we are lovers?' she demanded furiously. 'Tell me, Noah, do you always keep a fancy necklace handy in case your latest mistress doesn't have anything suitable to wear?' she snapped.

'Only married men have mistresses, Elizabeth.'

'Really? Then what do you have? A harem?'

'The same rule applies, I believe. Besides, I make every effort to devote myself to one woman at a time,' he said, a little drily.

'How noble. So how will you explain away your sudden interest in me to that French actress you've been so cosy with lately?'

'Simone?' He seemed amused. 'You can safely leave me to worry about that. Now turn around and I'll fasten this for you.'

He was not going to take no for an answer. He probably never had to. Tempting as it was to try for a sensational first, Lizzie turned. She just wanted to get the whole thing over with. And as he lifted the pendant over her head to fasten it about her throat she caught sight of the tall dark man framing her in the mirror. Olivia's brother had his own twisted reasons for what he was doing, but it would be some kind of balm to her own shattered pride if Peter believed that a man like Noah Jordan would want her to wear his jewels.

As he picked up one of the long earrings Lizzie held out her hand. 'I can do that. Your method of removing jewellery is a little drastic for comfort.' She carefully removed her pearl studs and Noah handed her the earrings without comment. 'Are these real?' she asked as she fastened the long drops to her ears.

'They are certainly not a figment of your imagination.'

'That's not what I meant. If they're real...' She shook her head. She was being ridiculous. It was a common enough practice to have copies made of fine jewels. The real ones probably never left the bank vault. She caught sight of Noah's mocking face reflected in the mirror and raised one shoulder a little awkwardly, wishing that she had never raised the subject. 'I ... just think ... I'd feel safer in paste.'

'Would you?' His answering smile was oddly humourless—a mere widening of the lips, a deepening of the lines that bit into his cheeks. It didn't touch the eyes that gleamed like old pewter in the evening light as he lifted the pendant from her throat and held it between his fingers.

'These jewels,' he said slowly, 'were made for a queen—the gift of a lover who thought he might be invited to share her throne as well as her bed. She kept the jewels . . . but his presumption cost him his head.' He paused, his head thrown back a little as he regarded her down the length of his aquiline nose.

'They've changed hands a good many times since then. Sometimes violently. Once on the turn of a card. Always at great cost. And always they have been worn by the most beautiful women of the age. Princesses . . .' He paused again. 'Courtesans. Even a silent-movie star— the gift of an Arab prince for who knows what favours . . .' She caught her breath. 'And now they lie against your skin, Elizabeth. So, tell me, how safe do you feel?'

The room had gone away. And the sunlight. She was conscious only of the light touch of his knuckles against her throat. And his eyes holding her captive, suspended in some place where there was no need to breathe.

'I . . . I shouldn't be wearing them,' she protested faintly. His fingers tightened momentarily about the pendant, then he laid it very gently back in the hollow of her neck. When he looked up again the dangerous expression in his eyes was eclipsed.

'Probably not,' he murmured carelessly. 'But they deserve one night off in five hundred years, don't you think?'

Lizzie gasped. Then overstretched nerves expressed themselves in a giggle. 'I thought you were supposed to be famous for your charm?' she said impetuously.

'Am I?' He was very still for a moment. 'And weren't you charmed? Just for a moment?' The faintest smile mocked her as the bright colour darkened her cheekbones. Of course she had been. He had said that he could have her eating out of his hand, and he had just proved it with his preposterous fairy-tale. But he had caught her off guard. It wouldn't happen again.

'Charm away, Mr Jordan,' she invited recklessly. 'I can see right through you. I'm immune.'

'In that case, Elizabeth, we should do very well together.' He extended a hand. 'Shall we go?' The hand was a challenge she could not ignore, and after only the slightest hesitation she laid her fingers upon his and allowed him to lead her out to the Bentley, where Harper was waiting to drive them to the theatre.

'So many people!' Lizzie exclaimed as the car disgorged them in front of the Coliseum.

'It's something of an occasion,' he agreed as they joined the throng of celebrities gathering in animated groups in the magnificent foyer.

The great columns of the theatre had been garlanded with flowers from floor to ceiling, and everywhere the atmosphere hummed with excitement. Noah was continuously hailed as they made their way through the crush, and she found herself the subject of many speculative glances as she was introduced to the kind of people she normally only saw in the newspapers or on television.

They made their way slowly through the throng, the black dress, the stunning jewels attracting their fair share of admiring glances, and Lizzie was a thousand times

thankful not to be wearing the embarrassment that would
have been her pink taffeta.

Then she saw Peter. He had abandoned classic English
tailoring for an Armani evening suit that did little for
his tall, slender figure, and he looked ill at ease, as if
he would rather be anywhere else. Clearly it was
Francesca who had insisted on their coming. And it was
Francesca who saw her first, her eyes widening slightly
at this very different vision of Lizzie from the bridesmaid
she had met that afternoon.

'Hello, Francesca, Peter. I'm so glad you decided to
come,' Noah said, from somewhere over her shoulder.

Why had she ever thought Peter was tall? Lizzie wondered as the two men shook hands. Peter was close to
six feet, Noah perhaps only two or three inches taller,
but his figure was broader, more commanding and
seemed to dwarf the younger man.

'Shall we go up?' Noah invited, and took Francesca's
arm. 'Tell me, have you been to London before,
Francesca?' he asked as he led the way.

'No. But I've always wanted to. My mother was
English.'

'Really? Tell me about her.'

'You look very...sophisticated, Lizzie,' Peter's voice
broke in a little awkwardly as they followed the other
couple. He didn't take her arm, and for that she was
oddly grateful. It made it so much easier to keep everything on a civilised footing. If he had touched her she
thought she might just have screamed. 'Very...grown-
up.' He left her in no doubt as to his meaning.

She took a deep breath. Time to start pretending. Not
for Noah, but for her own pride. 'I am grown-up, Peter.'

'Clearly. Perhaps I should have pressed a
little harder...'

Lizzie felt a jab of irritation that he could be so tactless with his wife just a few feet away. Not that Francesca was listening; she was too deeply engrossed in her conversation with Noah. 'Perhaps you weren't really that eager,' she retaliated. 'It didn't take you long to find someone else.'

'I waited—'

Noah turned, and she wondered if he had heard. His expression told her nothing as he bestowed a dazzling smile upon her. The ability to act, she thought, must run in the family. 'Enjoying yourself, darling?' he murmured.

She forced herself to smile back. 'I'm having a wonderful time. Darling,' she added as Noah's eyes prompted her.

'You always did love the opera,' Peter said as he turned away. 'I was going to bring you myself once.'

'For my eighteenth birthday.'

'Was it?' He frowned. 'Why—?'

'You went to Italy for the summer. You didn't come back in time.' It was getting easier, she found, to force the smiles. 'You sent me a postcard.'

'Florence is wonderful', he had written. 'I'm staying an extra week. You should have come with me'. And she had cried herself to sleep for a week because she had wanted to, more than anything else in the world. And he had forgotten his promise to take her to Covent Garden for her birthday. He hadn't even remembered to send her a card.

They arrived at their box and Noah ushered them all inside. There were chocolates and flowers—white roses for Fran, red for Lizzie—and exquisite, silk-embroidered programmes that Francesca exclaimed over.

'Will you sit here, Francesca?' Noah held the chair for her. 'And Elizabeth—you here, between us.' He took her hand and did not release it even when she was seated, entwining her fingers between his as if he could not bear to let them go. It was the tender gesture of a man in love, not to be missed, and Peter did not miss it. He took the remaining chair on the other side of his wife without comment, his mouth a tight, disapproving line.

The minute the lights went down Lizzie snatched her hand away. Undaunted, Noah draped his arm across the back of her chair. But she no longer cared. As the overture swelled she leaned forward, determined not to miss a note. There was no reason why she shouldn't enjoy the performance on stage, even if the one being enacted in the tight little world of their box made her feel slightly sick.

The music came at her in great waves, washing over her with drama, colour and passion, and for a while she could forget the dreadful day. It was something of a shock, when the lights came on for the interval, to find herself back in the awkward little circle.

'You and Noah seem to be quite an item,' Fran said as she whisked a comb through a soft cloud of dark hair in the powder room. 'To be honest, what with Peter's mother being so tight-lipped and you looking pretty knocked back this afternoon ... I thought that you and Peter might have had something going ...'

Lizzie swallowed. 'Is that why you married him before you flew to London?' She managed a pretty convincing laugh. She was proud of herself. 'Just in case he had a girl back home?'

'We've been married two months, Lizzie.' And to her astonishment Fran blushed. 'It was a rush job.' Confused thoughts crowded into Lizzie's head. Two months? That long? He'd been rushed into marrying this girl? He hadn't known that she was free ...

'You're pregnant?'

'The baby miscarried,' Fran said, 'two days after the wedding.' Her face clouded at this painful memory. Then she touched her waist protectively. 'But maybe this time...' Then she smiled at Lizzie. 'I haven't told Peter this time. He was so disappointed before...'

Unable to decide whether everything was infinitely worse or infinitely better, Lizzie kept smiling somehow. 'I hope everything will go well this time. Mrs Hallam will be thrilled to be a grandmother. She's been so looking forward—' Lizzie stopped before Fran wondered why she would have been discussing grandchildren with Mrs Hallam. 'But I thought you were married within the last day or two,' she said. 'Peter's mother never said a word when I saw her last week.'

'She didn't know. Your father's invitation arrived, and Peter thought it was a good opportunity to come over and tell his parents face to face.'

She should have been shocked, but oddly she was not. It didn't surprise her at all that Peter had opted to introduce his new wife to his parents surrounded by the entire village, thus avoiding a private and very sticky confrontation with his father. 'They were very kind,' Fran continued, 'considering...'

'Mrs Hallam is a dear. She'll soon get over the surprise. Especially once you tell her the good news.' She would have to. They all would.

'I wish I could be so sure.'

'Believe me, she's the kindest woman.'

Francesca smiled, obviously reassured to some extent. 'So,' she asked, 'when are you and Noah going to set a date?'

Lizzie was jolted out of her dark thoughts. 'Noah and I?' She stared at their reflections in the mirror, the contrast between her sophisticated black dress and Fran's scarlet frills. Fran might be her senior by two or three years, an investment analyst with a job at one of the world's great banks, but at the moment it was 'little' Lizzie French who looked the older, the wiser of the two. She felt it by a hundred years.

'Noah's not the marrying kind, Fran.' And the ripple of laughter that followed deserved an Academy award. 'But the sex is great.' And with that simple lie she let go of Peter and all the dreams she had cherished since he had fished her out of the village pond when she was six.

They were both laughing when they finally joined the men in the crush bar. Noah gave Lizzie a sharp look as he handed her the fruit juice she had asked for.

'What on earth have you two been talking about for so long?' Peter asked a little edgily.

'Girl-talk, honey,' Fran said, looping her arm in his and giving it a little squeeze. 'Lizzie has been telling me a few things about you that she thought I ought to know.'

'Really?' Noah asked, deeply interested. 'What sort of things?' Lizzie and Fran exchanged a glance and burst out laughing again. 'Don't rush your drinks, you two,' Noah said to Fran and Peter as the bell rang. 'You've got a couple of minutes.' And he took Lizzie's glass from her and placed it on the bar.

His grip on her elbow was deceptively firm as he steered her back to their box. 'You didn't waste any time making friends with the bride,' he said angrily, closing the door behind them.

'I like her,' she said.

'And it's so much easier to be near the husband when the wife likes you.'

Lizzie sighed. 'Doesn't all that moral outrage stick in your throat, Noah? You're no angel.'

'I've never messed with anyone's marriage.'

'A bit complicated, I expect, for someone of your advanced years.'

'I manage,' he said through gritted teeth, and without warning jerked her into his arms. 'I manage very well.'

No... The word formed on her lips but never disturbed the rose-scented air. Down in the auditorium the noise level began to rise as people returned to their seats, but up in the box, screened by the looped velvet curtains, the only sound was the tiniest gasp as his lips brushed hers with a teasing lightness that sent a fizz of adrenalin racing through her body.

No! The word panicked in her head, but her body wasn't listening. Instead her lids fluttered down over a pair of startled blue eyes and her own lips parted on a little sigh.

His tongue touched hers, for a moment lingered, tasting the sweetness of her mouth, then stroked masterfully along the length of it, sparking an electrifying response that carried her away on a roller coaster of wild sensations—shocking new feelings that made the blood sing in her veins. He tasted male—strong and exciting and dangerous. And she needed someone to love her, hold her, make her forget... Her lungs filled with the scent of him, and for a brief, crazy moment she was responding with unashamed passion.

'Should we have knocked?' Fran's amusement drove them apart, but far from being embarrassed Noah laughed softly, deep down in his throat, and dropped another light kiss upon Lizzie's mouth.

'It's the Puccini factor, Fran. Elizabeth tends to get rather carried away. She listens to him in bed...' He regarded her flaming cheeks without compassion. 'Don't you darling?' he insisted, his voice gentle but his eyes flint-hard.

She reached up and touched his cheek with the tips of her fingers. 'You've never complained,' she observed, and thoroughly enjoyed the jolt of surprise that widened his grey eyes. 'Have you, darling?'

'Perhaps you should know that I prefer Mozart,' he murmured, for her ears alone, and handed her back to her seat as, mercifully, the lights dimmed to disguise her heated cheeks.

Only when the curtain came down on the final act and she let out a long, slow breath did she realise that she was clutching Noah's hand, her fingers gripping so tightly that he was unable to withdraw it without disturbing her concentration. She just managed to stop herself from snatching her hand away. Then she saw the marks that her nails had made.

'Oh, Noah, I'm sorry.'

'Are you?' His voice was hardly audible, but he clearly thought that she had done it on purpose. 'Perhaps you should kiss it better,' he suggested, offering his palm.

Aware that Fran and Peter were watching this exchange with fascination, she touched his hand lightly with her finger. 'Later—I promise,' she murmured. Then the curtain was drawn back and the audience erupted in enthusiastic applause.

'Thank you so much, Noah, for the most wonderful evening,' Fran said as they collected their belongings.

'It isn't over unless you want it to be. I've a table booked at Annabel's.'

Dismay swept over Lizzie. She had done everything that he had asked of her—more. More than he would ever know. But it was as if he was intent on punishing her. She had been up since dawn, she was tired, and her head was stuffed with a day full of misery. But as Fran exclaimed with delight she knew that she had no choice but to play his game until the bitter end.

The crowd was beginning to thin a little, and Harper had the car waiting for them at the kerb as they emerged from the theatre. Noah helped Fran into the back, then Lizzie. Peter followed. 'I don't take up quite as much space as you, Noah,' he said. 'You'll be more comfortable in the front.'

Noah conceded gracefully but Lizzie, confined against Peter, sincerely wished he hadn't. With painful intensity the ride brought back memories of other times when they had squashed together in the back of someone's car, to go to a party, or to the cinema in Melchester. Then his arm would have been around her and he would have been laughing at something she had said. Now, as they swept through Trafalgar Square, he leaned across to Fran to point out the sights, knocking Lizzie's bag from her lap.

He retrieved it after a moment's fumbling on the floor of the car and handed it back to her. 'Sorry, Lizzie.'

'No problem,' she said. And somehow those four words said it all.

It was a relief when the car came to a halt in Berkeley Square. Then they were enveloped in the noisy atmosphere of the nightclub and speech was no longer a necessity. The champagne was broached, Noah proposed a toast to the newlyweds, then Fran pulled Peter onto the dance floor and they disappeared in the throng.

'In every relationship they say that one partner loves and the other is loved,' Noah remarked. 'I'd say Peter is a man who likes to be loved.'

'Then he should be happy with Fran. She loves him enough for two.'

'For some men that just isn't enough.'

'You should know.'

He ignored her remark, flipping open her evening bag to extract a small folded piece of paper between two fingers. 'Neat trick, but not very original.' He offered her the paper. 'What does he say?'

Lizzie shrank back, too horrified by the implication of the note even to touch it.

'I'll hazard a guess, shall I?' He stared at the paper as if he could see through it. '"I must see you"—' he looked up '—closely followed by instructions on how to achieve that aim. Of course—' he shrugged '—I may be wrong.'

She snatched the note from his fingers and dropped it into an ashtray. Then she tore a match from the complimentary book on the table, struck it and touched the flame to the paper. It burned briefly, the thin curl of smoke sharp in her nostrils, before it crumpled to ash. 'Now we'll never know, will we?'

Lizzie no longer needed Noah to drive her. Francesca had been easy to convince that they were lovers. Now she must be sure that Peter believed it too. Believed that even if he had been free she would no longer have been interested. She tried desperately to remember what she had said to him when he had arrived at the wedding.

'Just as well it was a short note,' Noah said drily, interrupting her thoughts, 'or you might have set off the sprinkler system. Shall we dance?' It wasn't an invitation to be taken lightly or refused. He was already on his feet, and she rose, too tired to go through with the ritual protest.

He folded her in his arms and they moved in time to the music. It wasn't dancing—the floor was too crowded for anything that positive—but it served his purpose. His hand at her back gathered her in against his lithe body, demonstrating quite effectively to anyone who was interested that she belonged to him. She didn't resist. Peter might be watching. Instead she put her arms about Noah's neck and leaned against him, resting her head against his shoulder.

For a while they moved together to the slow rhythm of the music and Lizzie felt an unexpected charge of excitement against the warmth of his body, his thighs moving against hers, his hands caressing her back. She leaned back in his arms and stared up at him.

'Kiss me, Noah,' she invited huskily.

He regarded her from dark, heavy-lidded eyes. 'You think making him jealous will bring him back?' His voice was soft, dangerous. She shook her head, too close to tears now to speak.

'Just kiss me.'

He hesitated, then briefly his lips touched hers, and in that moment she understood what was meant by 're-bound'. If they hadn't been in a crowded nightclub at that moment, she would willingly have fallen into Noah's bed.

'Elizabeth?' His fingers touched her cheek. 'You're crying.'

'Everyone cries at weddings, Noah. Didn't you know that?' She allowed him to mop her cheeks. It wouldn't do for Peter to suspect that she was anything but deliri-ously happy. But she had come to the end of her tether, and when they arrived back at their table to find Fran and Peter waiting for them, she was leaning against Noah more than convincingly.

'I'm afraid jet lag has caught up with us, Noah. I hope you don't mind us deserting you?' Peter said, ap-parently unable even to look at Lizzie.

'On the contrary—it's been a long day all round. We'll drop you at your hotel.'

As they pulled up in Albemarle Street Fran said, 'Can we meet some time this week, Lizzie? Perhaps go shopping?' Lizzie hesitated. She liked Fran, but wasn't sure that she could cope with the complications of such a friendship.

'Make it Thursday,' Noah intervened. 'Elizabeth will take you to Fortnum's and indoctrinate you in the art of the British tea ceremony. And I've a new exhibition opening in the evening. You can both come and join us for dinner afterwards.'

The sun was already high when Mrs Harper finally drew back the curtains to let in the day. 'I'm sorry to wake you, Miss Lizzie, but Mr Jordan said not to leave you any later.'

'What time is it?' She struggled up from the pillow, blinking sleepily through heavy eyes, her head throbbing.

'Just after ten. Mr Jordan had his breakfast hours ago and he's gone down to the gallery, so I've brought you a tray and the papers. There's a lovely picture of Miss Olivia... I'll have to get used to calling her Mrs French now, won't I?' She laughed a little self-consciously. 'And your father, of course. Such a distinguished man. It's in that one—' she indicated one of the papers '—and one of you and Mr Jordan in those two.' She straightened. 'He said to tell you that he'll be taking you out to lunch.'

'Did he?' Then she supposed he would. He seemed to get everything he wanted, but the sooner she found somewhere to live the better, she thought, picking up the first of the papers. The marriage of a well-known actress always interested the Press, and there had been a group of photographers outside the church. Noah, too, was a favourite, but she was surprised that they had printed a photograph of her.

Mrs Harper withdrew, and Lizzie poured herself a cup of tea and began to leaf through. The wedding had made a bit of a splash on the inside pages, but there was no picture of her, or Noah. She shrugged and flicked through the second paper. But it wasn't a photograph of the wedding that caught her eye.

It was a photograph of Noah, his hand at her back, escorting her into the theatre. There was a brief caption—'Noah Jordan arriving at a charity gala last night with his house guest, the beautiful Elizabeth French.' She remembered that he had paused briefly to exchange a word with someone, introduce her. There had been so many flashes that she had not noticed a camera pointed specifically at them.

Her brows drew together in a tiny frown. The photograph made her look different somehow. The soft material of the black dress emphasised her figure as it clung to curves that she had always thought rather boyish, and the jewels at her throat and ears added to the illusion of sophisticated womanhood.

If it had been a photograph of another woman she would have been convinced that they were— House guest! It didn't take much intelligence to work out who had told the journalist that. It was one thing convincing Peter and Fran that they were lovers; did he have to invite the whole world to share in the deception?

With a little snap of anger she dropped the paper. She went into the bathroom and stood under a fierce shower jet until she felt more like herself. Then she dressed in a pair of blue jeans and a plain white T-shirt and, leaving her hair loose about her shoulders, surveyed her reflection.

'The beautiful Elizabeth French' indeed! Not this morning, with eyes red-rimmed from the hours spent shedding tears into her pillow. A little make-up helped. But it would be Lizzie French that Noah took out to lunch today, not some *femme fatale* that he had created out of Olivia's leftovers.

She picked up her tray and carried it downstairs, heading for the back of the house in search of the kitchen.

'You needn't have brought that down!' Mrs Harper exclaimed as she opened the door.

'I'm not used to being waited on, Mrs Harper. But I was wondering if you had last week's evening papers?' She could make a start on finding somewhere temporary to live while she looked around.

'Well, there's the Friday edition. Will that do?'

'It's a start. Is there somewhere I can use a telephone?'

'Use the morning room, Miss Lizzie.' She pointed her in the right direction and left her to it.

The morning room was fresh and bright, with French windows standing open to an inviting courtyard garden. It was decorated in pale blues and greens and furnished for comfort rather than elegance with an overstuffed sofa and a couple of chintz-covered armchairs, one of which was occupied by a large and very battered cat who opened an eye and regarded her stonily for a moment, daring her to make any claim upon his chair. Apparently satisfied that he had made his point, he closed it again.

Lizzie tickled his ear and then dropped the paper on a small desk that occupied a corner. She found some notepaper and a pen and began to work her way through the small ads offering accommodation, noting anything that might possibly do.

The first flat had already been let when she telephoned. She dialled the second number on her list and it began to ring. The phone was answered by a man. 'Good morning,' she said, 'I'm ringing about the advert for a flat—'

The phone went dead. Lizzie stared at it, shook it, then pressed the handset button. Nothing. Then, sensing that she was no longer alone, she spun around in the

chair. Noah was leaning against the doorway with the
other end of the telephone connection in his hand.

'You'll need a jacket, Elizabeth,' he drawled. 'I'll be
waiting for you in the car.'

CHAPTER FOUR

LIZZIE'S protest died on her lips. Noah hadn't waited to hear it. Besides, she had come somewhat painfully to the conclusion that she would never get the better of him by direct confrontation. So, she would let him take her out to lunch. Tomorrow he had a gallery to run, and she would be free to do as she pleased. And she would be very pleased to leave his house.

The only jacket she had with her was a navy blazer, but it looked surprisingly good with the jeans and T-shirt. She still had the silk chiffon scarf and wrapped it around her head bandeau-style, then scowled at her reflection. If she had hoped to annoy him with her choice of clothes she had gone wide of the mark. Despite the jeans, she looked oddly stylish.

He made no comment on her appearance, however. Perhaps because he was wearing a pair of close-fitting denims himself, and a well-rubbed leather bomber jacket that had certainly seen better days. He was leaning against the huge silver Bentley, arms folded, regarding the toe of his shoe as if it held the answer to the world's problems, and for just a moment she hesitated in the doorway, startled by an unexpected feeling of warmth for the man. Then he glanced up.

'At last.' He opened the car door for her.

'I'm sure you're used to waiting for women, Noah,' she said, sweeping past him with all the poise she could muster.

'The results are usually worth waiting for,' he replied as he shut the door on her. She pushed the seatbelt strap

61

home with rather more force than was necessary, surprised how much that remark had hurt. She had doubtless asked for it, but he didn't have to be quite so frank.

She kept her eyes straight ahead as he started the car and headed south towards the river, leaving it to Noah to reopen hostilities or not as he chose. It wasn't long before he broached the subject on his mind. 'What's the rush to move on, Elizabeth?' he asked, with every appearance of amiability. She was not deceived. 'Has my charm faded so quickly?'

'What charm?' she asked, and this time was rewarded with a tightening of his lips that might—just—have been described as a smile in acknowledgement of her strike. She lifted her shoulders a little awkwardly. 'The truth is, Noah, I don't care to be described as your "house guest" in the Sunday newspapers.'

'But you are,' he reasoned, his smile deepening at her discomfiture.

'Me and a cast of thousands.'

'That impertinent tongue will get you into serious trouble one of these days. Some people aren't as tolerant—' He broke off, clearly exasperated with her. 'Just tell me what you're looking for in the way of a flat and my secretary will find some for you to look at.'

This was too much. 'I'm quite capable of finding somewhere to live, Noah.'

'Really?' His voice was cutting. 'Shall we run through the method? You ring a number advertised in the newspaper. You have no idea what the area is like, but a nice young man says "Come around and have a look". And you go. On your own. Have I got it right?'

Put like that it sounded positively reckless. 'That's the way most people—'

'No. Only ignorant young girls who know no better. No wonder your father was so insistent—' He stopped abruptly, apparently too annoyed with her to continue. 'Have you any idea which part of London you want to live in?' he asked.

'No. I just want something temporary while I look for a job—'

'You've already got somewhere temporary,' he interjected. 'As I know to my cost.'

She ignored this. 'Then I'll look around for something to buy,' she continued.

'Buy?' She had clearly taken him by surprise. 'You don't want much, do you? Or is that your price for leaving Olivia and James in peace?'

Lizzie stared at him. Whatever kind of monster had Olivia painted her as? She snapped her head back to stare through the windscreen, dismissing any attempt to convince him that she was... what? 'I'm a good girl, I am.' Eliza Doolittle's plaintive wail popped into her head. No. If you had to say it, it didn't mean anything. And she told herself that it didn't matter one jot what Noah Jordan thought of her.

'Dad is going to need every penny he can raise for his new...responsibilities. I have a little money of my own.'

'Enough to buy a flat in London?' he demanded.

If she wasn't too fussy, she thought. But that was none of his business. 'How's *your* bank balance, Noah?' she probed, flashing a glance from bright blue eyes. 'You tell me how much you're worth and I might repay the compliment.'

He regarded her thoughtfully. 'It's a good time to buy,' he said. 'Not such a good time for job-hunting, though.'

'I'll get a job,' she said.

'Eventually. With a little help from me.'

This casual dismissal riled Lizzie. 'Surely you wouldn't wish me on any of your friends?' she enquired a little waspishly, but she didn't wait for the answer. 'I assure you I am quite capable of getting a job on my own initiative.'

'Are you indeed?' He turned a pair of forceful grey eyes upon her. 'What as, I wonder?'

What indeed? Not that she had wasted her time during the past five years. As well as being a competent cook, she could type and was an efficient bookkeeper, keeping her father one step ahead of the tax man and VAT inspector, and she was treasurer for a local charity. 'I'll think of something,' she assured him. 'I'm not totally unemployable.'

'Would you care to make a small wager on that?'

'Why keep it small? Make it as big as you like,' she invited, feeling reckless.

'A proper job,' he warned. 'Nothing temporary, and I won't consider dishing out hamburgers in a fast-food chain,' he insisted. 'A job that will support you and offer some prospects.'

'You don't want much, do you?' she asked.

'What's the matter? Scared of a challenge?'

'Certainly not.'

Apparently satisfied, he smiled. It was not, however, reassuring. 'Then we'd better decide on the stakes.'

'When I get a job you can take me to see *Aida*,' she said, naming the first opera that came into her head.

'It's not on this season's repertoire,' he objected.

Lizzie hadn't thought of that but she wasn't going to let him off the hook. 'If it's too difficult you could always back out,' she offered tormentingly.

He took a deep breath, as if barely holding onto his temper. 'No, I'll think of something. *Aida* it is. Now, the big question is what will you do for me if *I* win?'

His eyes flickered over her briefly, and Lizzie felt her cheeks grow warm. Surely he wouldn't...? 'I think you'll have to give up wearing jeans,' he said, and his taunting eyes told her that he knew exactly what she had been thinking.

'That's not fair,' she blustered, to cover her blushes. 'You're wearing jeans.'

'They are working clothes.' And a broad grin unexpectedly lit his face. 'Unlike you, I haven't been lying in bed all morning.'

She swallowed, wishing that she had never started to bait him. It was a game that he was able to win every time and she would do well to remember that and keep her mouth shut. 'Will I have to give them up for ever?' she asked quickly.

'That's not a condition I'm in any position to enforce. While you're staying with me will do.'

She shrugged. 'Well, that's no imposition,' she replied, well satisfied with her bargain. 'I don't intend staying for long.'

'You'll stay until you get a job,' he insisted. 'And somewhere suitable to live.' She didn't bother to argue. But she didn't agree either. They had arrived at St Katherine's Dock, and he pulled into a parking space near the marina. 'But, for the purposes of our bet, you have until close of business next Saturday.' He offered his hand to seal the bargain. 'Agreed?'

'A week?' she protested. 'That's not very long.'

'If it's too difficult you are perfectly free to back out,' he advised her, and he lifted his dark brows a taunting fraction.

Impetuously she placed her hand in his. 'Agreed.' He grasped her hand in his broad palm momentarily, but when he released it she let out a little gasp.

'What is it?'

Lizzie didn't answer, but gently traced the row of red marks left by her nails with the tip of her finger. She had promised him that she would kiss it better, and on an impulse she bent to drop a kiss on his palm. For a moment there was silence. When she looked up his eyes were shaded, yet she was sure that her whimsical gesture had shaken him. Well, that was hardly surprising. She had shaken herself. 'I promised,' she muttered awkwardly. 'Better late than never.'

'Maybe. I'll let you know. Are you hungry?' he asked. 'Or shall we walk for a while?'

Thankful that he hadn't dwelt on a gesture that she hardly understood herself, she said, 'I'd like to walk, please. I had a late breakfast.'

'Ten o'clock? On a Sunday? The crack of dawn, I promise you.'

'You were up a great deal earlier,' she reminded him.

'There was nobody to keep me in bed,' he replied softly, and she snatched her hand away from his, blushing to the roots of her hair.

'I'm sorry if I'm cramping your lifestyle, Noah. If you had taken me to Islington...'

'Forget Islington,' he commanded, and, swinging his long legs out of the car, he walked around and opened the door for her. 'And you can safely leave me to worry about the way I run my life.' He shrugged. 'Right now I'm in the middle of organising a new exhibition, and there are always last-minute details to sort out. Sunday is a good day for that. No interruptions.'

'Not even from your French actress?'

'For a girl apparently addicted to the gossip columns you are remarkably ignorant. Simone returned to France last week to start work on a film.' He slung his jacket over his shoulder.

Lizzie blushed again. 'Oh. I'm sorry.'

'There's no need to be, Elizabeth.' His smile was wolfish. 'It leaves me with so much more time to devote to you.'

'Is she coming back soon?' Lizzie asked hopefully.

'Sorry,' he said, with a grin. 'I won't see Simone again until the next time she and her husband are looking for someone to finance—'

'Husband? But you said you never... Oh!'

'Would you care to change the subject, Elizabeth?' he invited. 'Or would you like a blow-by-blow account of how I met them when they bought a Matisse last year? Or maybe you are more interested in how I introduced them to some friendly bankers with the money to back their film, or how I just happened to be the one they didn't cut out of the photograph when the three of us went out to celebrate—'

'No!' Lizzie held up a hand to stop him. She'd got the picture. 'I'd rather you told me about your new exhibition,' she suggested.

'New American artists. Fran should enjoy it,' he added a little slyly. 'You'd better give some thought to the dinner party afterwards, since you'll be hostess. There'll be twelve of us altogether.'

'Sorry, Noah, I'll be far too busy job-hunting. And flat-hunting.'

'I thought you might like to start with the quenelles you made for dinner the other evening,' he said, ignoring her objection.

'You liked them?'

He regarded her with amusement. 'Have I touched your vanity, Elizabeth? Perhaps you should consider a career in—'

'That does seem to be the general consensus of opinion,' she snapped. And maybe they were all right, she thought. She had certainly better start considering the matter very seriously indeed if she was going to get a job by the end of the week.

They continued walking along the edge of the marina, listening to the ropes clanging noisily in the rigging of the yachts and watching the general bustle as the boats left their moorings. Noah pointed out several craft that belonged to well-known personalities.

'Do you have a boat?' she asked.

He regarded her with a slightly jaundiced expression. 'What did you have in mind? Something very large, with a little house on top and a giraffe looking out of the window?'

'What...?' Then her cheeks grew warm. 'Oh, Lord, I didn't mean...'

He took pity on her confusion. 'It's all right. I'm afraid being born on an island in the middle of the Thames during a flood is apt to make one a little sensitive on the subject of boats. But no, I don't have anything larger than an outboard dinghy down at the cottage. Even if I was so inclined, I'm away too much for it to be worthwhile.'

'Where do you go?'

'Wherever works of art are being bought or sold. New York at least once a month, and I've been in Eastern Europe a lot during the past couple of years—Prague, St Petersburg, Budapest, even Moscow. A lot of art has turned up since the break-up of the USSR. Someone has to authenticate it.'

He paused to watch the comings and goings of people on the boats. The breeze coming off the river ruffled the immaculate cut of his thick dark hair and billowed the soft linen of his shirt in stark contrast to the way his faded blue denims clung to strong, well-muscled thighs. He had turned back the cuffs of his shirt, and as he leaned on the rails Lizzie's eyes were drawn irresistibly to the sleek line of fine dark hairs that moulded and emphasised the sinewy power of his arms.

'I'd love to travel,' Lizzie said, looking quickly away.

'Then perhaps you should try and get a job with an airline,' he advised, with every appearance of sincerity.

'Oh, that's not travelling.'

He turned his head to glance at her, his dark, well-marked brows rising slightly in query.

'Travelling is a dusty road disappearing into the distance. Not knowing what you'll find at the end of it, and not being in any great hurry to find out because there are so many interesting things to see on the way.'

'Scratch any modern girl and you'll find a romantic. It never ceases to amaze me. But when it comes right down to it I find that most of them prefer first class.'

'Well, you've scratched more than most, I dare say,' she responded impulsively. 'So you're probably an authority.'

He grasped her elbow and led her across to a wine bar, where the chairs and tables had spilled out onto the pavement, and sat her down rather firmly. 'Perhaps lunch will give your mouth something useful to do.'

She opened her mouth to retaliate, then closed it again quickly. There was a blackboard leaning against the wall and she fixed it with a furious eye. Not that she was taking in anything that was written upon it. Instead she fumed helplessly at the insufferable rudeness of the man. But then, she hadn't been exactly polite herself. And she had promised herself that she wouldn't allow him to provoke her into further unguarded responses. She just couldn't seem to help herself.

'Well?' he enquired after a while.

'A *salade niçoise*, please,' she said.

'And then?'

'I'm not very hungry.'

He turned to the waiter. 'Smoked salmon with horse-radish, a *salade niçoise*, and two fillet steaks, very rare...' He ordered wine and, before she could utter a word of protest, said, 'You didn't eat any of the supper Mrs Harper left for us last night.'

'I was too tired to eat.' And too miserable.

'If you're to start job-hunting tomorrow, you'll need to keep your strength up.'

The dangerous spark of annoyance that immediately leapt to her eye made him laugh, and suddenly she was laughing too.

'You are the most... infuriating man I've ever met,' she declared roundly.

'I'm the *only* man you've ever met,' he responded, with somewhat jaundiced conviction.

'I don't know what you mean,' she declared, then faltered momentarily under the challenge of quizzing grey eyes. The truth was, she knew only too well what he meant. She had thought that Peter was a man, but measured against the self-assurance, the ruthless determination of Noah Jordan...

Oh, Peter! Why on earth did you have to overreact so...? Lizzie gave a little sigh. He'd always been the same—inclined to drama when he couldn't get his own way. He'd arrived at her father's wedding with his new wife on his arm, determined that she should see what she had lost. Thanks to Noah he had been thwarted. And he clearly wasn't happy with the thought that someone else had apparently got what he had never had.

She wasn't sure whether she was angry with him or herself, for being able to see him so clearly. Love was supposed to be blind. She supposed it had been, but suddenly the rose-tinted glasses had become all too painfully clear.

Noah poured her a glass of wine, not bothering to contradict her. 'Try this,' he instructed. She sipped the pale golden liquid without comment. 'Well?'

'Oh, it's fine, thank you.' Then, after a moment, she added, 'Did you see Olivia's photograph in the newspaper this morning?'

'Did you see yours?' he countered. She pulled a face. 'You didn't like it? I thought it made you look very...sophisticated.'

'Too sophisticated. I didn't like the implication.'

'And what implication was that?' She didn't answer, but her look spoke volumes. 'Ah, the implication that you are, on the surface at least, a desirable young woman?' He leaned forward and stroked the edge of his thumb along the line of her jaw before hooking it under her chin so that she was forced to meet his probing eyes. 'The kind of woman that a man would want to take to his bed. Why should that worry you?'

'You believe I should be flattered because it's your bed I'm supposed to be occupying?'

'I don't suffer from that kind of conceit, Elizabeth.'

She swallowed hard. 'That's just as well, because it's the implication that it's *your* bed that bothers me most. And the fact that you must have told the newspaper—'

'On the contrary, you told their columnist yourself when I introduced him—' She started. 'Yes, I can see that you recall him without difficulty,' he said as she remembered the attractive young man they had spoken to in the foyer of the theatre.

'Why on earth didn't you warn me?' she demanded.

'It wouldn't have made any difference. Even without the caption...' He shrugged. 'A picture is worth a thousand words.'

'And it suited your purpose admirably.' She was furious.

'As you say... but since it isn't true why should it worry you?'

'Because other people will believe it. People I know.'

'Really?' He raised his eyebrows. 'Why should they do that unless your behaviour in the past would lead them to suppose—'

'My behaviour has nothing to do with it!'

'—that you might leap into my bed, should I be inclined to invite you to share it?' he continued, as if she hadn't spoken. 'Your father, for instance? Or Olivia? And all those good people back home who think you're such a dear, sweet girl?'

'No!'

'No. Of course not. They will read the words and take them at face value because they know, or think they know—which amounts to the same thing—just what you are like. As for the rest—the thousands who might construe some other meaning—does it matter? They don't know you and never will.' He stretched a pair of seemingly endless long legs out in front of him. 'There is a wise old saying, Elizabeth—Believe nothing that you read and only half of what you see. I commend it to you.'

'And what you hear?' She could have bitten out her tongue as his eyes narrowed sharply.

'And just what have you heard?' But before he could pursue this the waiter arrived with their lunch. By the time they had been served, Lizzie had gathered her wits and launched into a series of questions about the exhibition he was planning.

'What would you like to do this afternoon?' he asked later as they made their way back to the car.

'Please don't feel you have to entertain me.'

'Unfortunately I do. Although it appears to be more a question of keeping you out of mischief than entertaining you. I thought we might drive down to Windsor.'

'Did you indeed? And what do you plan to do for the rest of the week, while you're working—shackle me to the bed?'

He raised his brows slightly at the challenge in her voice. 'Don't tempt me,' he warned. 'Or I just might.'

She backed off, swung around and, stuffing her hands hard into her blazer pockets, began to walk swiftly away from him. She had no idea where she was going—it didn't matter just as long as it was far away from Noah. But his long stride easily overtook her, and before she could escape his arm was looped around her waist, pulling her close, forcing her to stop. 'You're going the wrong way,' he informed her.

'Leave me alone,' she said through clenched teeth. 'I've done nothing to deserve this.'

'Then why did Peter Hallam slip a note into your handbag last night?'

'Why don't you ask him? I have absolutely no desire to see him. You're the one who keeps throwing us together.'

'I don't believe you, Elizabeth, but for the next three days you have your desire.' She stared at him. 'Francesca expressed a wish to go to Stratford. I've arranged it for them. They won't be back until late on Wednesday evening.'

'Why?' She was puzzled, really puzzled as to why he should take such a personal interest. 'You scarcely know them.'

'Should you only do good turns for friends? Besides, Francesca...' He shrugged. 'She deserves a break.'

'Does she? Why?' Lizzie was almost certain that he had been going to say something else, but he didn't respond to her probing. 'She's tougher than she looks, Noah. Besides, Peter chose *her*. Married *her*. I'm the one who should be throwing hysterics.'

'That, Elizabeth, has been bothering me. Why aren't you?'

'Because...' She didn't know. 'Because I haven't had ten seconds to think about it, that's why,' she said crossly. 'Windsor, you said? Shall we go?' And she shook him off and headed swiftly back to the car.

What he planned to do in Windsor, she didn't ask. She expected nothing more exciting than a walk along by the river, or to wander around the castle. But he took her to Smith's Lawn in Windsor Great Park to watch a polo match, and they were quickly absorbed into a crowd of noisy spectators who welcomed Noah enthusiastically, accepting Lizzie without question as part of their charmed circle.

It was fast and thrilling, and Lizzie was swept along by the excitement, so that when they headed back on the motorway into London she found herself thanking Noah without any hesitation for the afternoon's entertainment. Until she saw the grim set of his jaw. After that she kept quiet.

The telephone was ringing in the hall as she walked through the front door. Noah had driven the car straight round to the garage, and for a moment Lizzie stared at the phone, wondering whether or not she should answer it. Then, since there was no one else to do it, she picked it up.

'Hello?'

'Lizzie! I've been waiting for you to ring me all day. Didn't you find my note?'

'Hello, Peter,' she said evenly, not betraying by the slightest tremor the way her spirits had sunk at the sound of his voice. 'What note?' she asked.

'The note... Oh, never mind. Look, I've got to see you.'

'Peter... please,' she begged.

'I want to know what the hell you're doing living with a man like Noah Jordan. Have you gone completely insane? The man's a heartbreaker, for heaven's sake; everybody knows that. You never let me so much... And now you're shacked up with—'

She put the phone down, and, dragging in a long, shuddering breath, turned to run for the sanctuary of her room, to stand under a hard shower and wash those words away. She blundered blindly into Noah instead. He caught her arms, steadied her.

'Good God, I can't leave you for a moment, can I?' Then, as he saw how pale she was, he swore very softly. 'Come on.' He pushed her into the drawing room and, without letting go of her for a moment, poured her a brandy. 'Drink this.' She didn't want it—the fumes caught at her throat, choking her—but he was adamant. Reluctantly she took a sip and the spirit heated her, jolted her back to life.

'I'm sorry, Noah. He was just so... angry.'

'Are you surprised? You must have been crazy to ring him at his hotel.'

'No!' She jerked free.

'Don't make it worse by lying, Elizabeth. He's married to someone else, and the sooner you accept it the better. You'll get over it eventually.'

Over it? She was halfway there already. It had been bad enough when he refused to understand why she couldn't marry him at the drop of a hat and go back to New York with him. He had known that she loved him and that should have been enough. She had waited for him long enough. But that he had been selfishly prepared to risk another girl's happiness... Still was...

'More advice, Noah?' She turned and handed him the crystal goblet, the brandy scarcely touched, but her attempt at a smile was undermined by the tears sparkling in her eyes. 'You should write an agony column; you're certainly a major pain...' And this time when she hurried from the room he made no attempt to stop her.

She fled almost by instinct to the kitchen. But it was a strange kitchen—clinical and efficient—nothing like the warm, inviting kitchen at Dove Court. There was no comfort to be found there, but rather than retreat to her room and risk running into Noah once more she went out into the garden, and curled up on an old seat hidden from the house by a tangle of rambling roses. It was quiet there. She would hardly have known that she was in London except for the occasional distant sound of a siren or car horn intruding above the bird-song.

For a while she tried to sort out her disordered thoughts. But she was too angry to think straight—angry with Peter. He had hurt her. Gone out of his way to hurt her. He could have written and told her the situation, but to turn up at her father's wedding without any warning... What his poor mother must have thought, being put in a position of having to welcome this unexpected daughter-in-law publicly at the biggest social event in the village since... She gave a little sigh. It didn't matter any more.

But her anger with Noah was a different thing. Other people found her straightforward, easy to get on with. At the polo match she had made friends with several of the girls; one had even offered to help her with flat-hunting and promised to ring her in the week. Noah had seemed to resent this. What had he called her? 'Miss

Sweetness'. She pulled a face. Whatever he had meant, it certainly hadn't been a compliment. He'd acted as if she'd had two heads and he had been the only one who could see it.

The cat found her, jumping up beside her on the seat and making a fuss. 'You're an unlikely resident of this house, mog,' Lizzie said, stroking the battered head. 'You should be something rare and exotic—an elegant Siamese, perhaps.'

'He isn't a resident at all. He lives next door. The trouble is he doesn't appear to know that.'

She hadn't heard Noah's approach across the grass, but now she looked up. 'You seem to be plagued by unwanted guests.'

'Nothing is allowed to plague me, Elizabeth.' He scooped up the cat and dumped him on the lawn, stretching out beside her on the seat.

'It was never my intention to impose upon you, Noah,' she said stiffly. 'I'll start flat-hunting in earnest tomorrow.'

'If you insist. I'll get my secretary onto it first thing.'

'There's no need, really.'

'Indulge me, Elizabeth. I promised your father I would look after you.'

'You have my assurance that it's not a life sentence,' she said, and received a chilling glance for her pains. 'Why do you insist on calling me Elizabeth?' she asked.

'You'd like me to call you Lizzie? Or even "little" Lizzie, perhaps. Like Peter Hallam?' She didn't answer. He was being deliberately insulting. 'Well?'

'Not like that.'

'Not any way, Elizabeth. It's time you grew up and stopped hiding behind a little girl's name.'

She regarded him with astonishment. 'What on earth do you think I'm hiding from?'

'Life in general. I can see why it suited your father to keep you at home as an unpaid housekeeper when your contemporaries were out in the world enjoying the temptations and hardships of life. What I can't understand is why you would put up with it. Waiting around in the hopes that Peter would come home and carry you off is hardly sufficient excuse.'

'I wasn't hanging around for anything. Peter asked me to marry him when he was at home at Christmas.'

If she had hoped to make his jaw drop she was disappointed. 'You weren't wearing a ring.' He didn't believe her.

'No,' she said, hoping that he would leave it at that, but he made an impatient gesture. 'We...quarrelled.'

'So you sent him an invitation to the wedding as an olive branch.' He stood up, walked a few feet then swung round, his eyes like slate in the gathering dusk. 'And he came.' He stared at her as if seeing her for the first time. 'My God, he came. You must be quite a performer under that virginal exterior. Have you no feelings to spare for Francesca?'

'She'll be all right, Noah; I—' Lizzie squealed as he grabbed her wrist and yanked her to her feet.

'You callous little bitch, I know exactly what you've got in mind. I heard you pleading with him to come back to you.'

'Noah,' she begged, 'please listen; I didn't—'

'No, you listen to me,' he demanded, overriding her, refusing to hear her out. 'I thought you had accepted the situation. You seemed to be making an effort. Despite everything Olivia had told me about you, I was still taken in by that innocent expression,' he said, oceans deep in self-disgust.

He took a deep breath in an effort to control his anger, and when he spoke again his voice dripped ice. 'Peter

Hallam might be regretting his hasty marriage, but impending fatherhood will concentrate his mind, providing you do nothing to distract him—'

'How do you know Francesca's pregnant?'

He didn't answer. 'What a pair you are.' His disgust was palpable. 'Frankly I think you deserve each other, but Francesca and her baby must come first. He is going to have to live with the results of his actions and so are you. But, since it is now clear that I can't trust you to behave with honour, I'll have to do something about it myself.'

'What are you going to do?' she demanded, tugging vainly at her wrist in an attempt to free herself from his grasp. 'I warn you, Noah, your make-believe affair has gone far enough—'

'Then we'll have to stop playing at make-believe, won't we?' He was very still. 'And start playing it for real.'

'What...?' Without apparent effort he began to draw her closer, until she could feel the heat of his body through the soft linen of his shirt, the steady beat of his heart under her fingers as she tried to hold him at bay. Then his free hand was at her back, pinning her against him, and she knew with the most ominous certainty that he was going to make love to her.

Except that there would be no love. What he was doing was cold-blooded, utterly calculating, because he believed that no matter how much she protested in the end she would succumb more than willingly to his embrace. He had demonstrated that power when he'd kissed her in the theatre and briefly she had been swept away. And he thought that she and Peter had been lovers. Was that what was in his mind—to overwrite her memories... make her forget?

She gasped as the reality of what was happening struck home, knowing just how easy it would be simply to surrender to this man and let him obliterate Peter from her memory. How easy... Already he was more real than Peter had ever been...

With a cry like a small, trapped animal Lizzie began a fierce and silent struggle, and he indulged her, allowing her to rage against him, her fists raining impotently against his broad chest and shoulders—a demonstration of the futility of her opposition to his will.

And all the time he held her close, so that the sensitive tips of her breasts brushed against his chest, her abdomen pressed against the frightening, tormenting, thrilling arousal of his loins, and her denim-clad legs met the solid resistance of a pair of hard thighs, forcing her to confront the memory of her reaction to his kiss.

When she was quite out of breath, shaking and weak in his arms and beyond further resistance, he released her.

Taken utterly by surprise, she staggered back and almost fell into the garden seat. She made no effort to move, to run, to escape. She was shaking so violently that she couldn't have taken a step without collapsing. But he was pitiless. No brandy this time. Instead he regarded her with total dislike.

'Relax, Elizabeth,' he drawled. 'I have no intention of taking you to my bed, willingly or unwillingly.'

'Not the action of a gentleman?' she demanded, but her voice shook so much that the bitter sarcasm was lost. 'Especially when you've promised Dad you'll take care of me,' she added.

His lips were compressed into a hard, straight line. 'Someone has to. And I'm it. And since I have no desire to invite witnesses to a bedroom farce I am left with only one alternative—I shall have to marry you.'

CHAPTER FIVE

LIZZIE stared at him in astonishment for a moment, then somewhat weakly she laughed. 'Don't be ridiculous.'

He didn't seem to hear. 'Wednesday is the first day possible. We'll have to go to the register office tomorrow morning to make the arrangements.'

'Noah, you're not listening to me. I have absolutely no intention of marrying you on Wednesday or—'

'Thursday might be better,' he agreed, with absolute seriousness.

'Or any other day,' she insisted.

'I've got an appointment first thing, but after that I'm free until the evening,' he continued, disregarding her objection.

'Well, I'm very sorry, Noah,' she said, fuming at the sheer matter-of-factness of the man. 'I *am* busy on Thursday. Or had you forgotten that you had arranged for me to shop with Francesca, followed by a tea party, the opening of your exhibition and the little matter of twelve guests for dinner?'

'No, I hadn't forgotten.' And he smiled. He actually smiled.

Not that it was one of those slay-'em-in-the-aisles kind of smiles that he reserved for people he actually liked, that he used to demonstrate just how irresistible he could be when he chose to exert his charm. Oh, no. This smile never reached his eyes at all. It was all mouth and white, even teeth, and for the first time in her life Lizzie understood the urge to wipe the smile from someone's face.

But before she could do just that he leaned forward, his hands on either side of her caging her against the bench, and she shrank back, desperate to put the maximum distance between them.

'I'm sure that under the circumstances Francesca will be more than understanding,' he said softly. 'You see, the great thing about having the ceremony on Thursday, Elizabeth, is that she and Peter will be back from Stratford. We can... No, *you* can invite them to be our witnesses.' He regarded her without compassion. 'What could be more perfect?'

He was serious. He really meant it. That humourless smile was still in place, but a pair of chilling grey eyes ran alarm bells in her head. She eased herself upright, taking care not to touch him. 'Don't you think Fran might just wonder about my lack of enthusiasm?' she offered carefully. 'Besides, you've the new exhibition opening on Thursday.'

'News of our wedding will bring the crowds flocking to the gallery, my dear. Everyone will want to meet you.' He straightened, and Lizzie breathed a sigh of relief as he turned away with a dismissive gesture. 'I'm sure any lack of enthusiasm on your part will be put down to simple nerves.'

'Of course. I should have thought of that. Any girl would be nervous marrying a man with your track record.'

'I'm beginning to find your constant, uninformed reference to my "track record" very irritating, Elizabeth. I'm thirty-one years old, and whilst I may not have lived the life of a monk I've done little to be ashamed of.'

'Marrying me would put that claim severely to the test.'

'On the contrary,' he said abruptly.

Lizzie raised her hand to her forehead. '"It is a far, far better thing that I do..."' she quoted dramatically.

'I wonder if you'll find it quite so amusing on Thursday morning?' he enquired, but clearly didn't expect an answer as he immediately continued, 'I think we'd better go inside and consider the most appropriate way of breaking the happy news to your father.'

'There is *no* appropriate way. And, since I have absolutely no intention of marrying you, it isn't necessary.' But she stood up anyway. 'If you'll excuse me, Noah, I'm leaving now.'

For a moment he blocked her path, his powerful figure threatening, his eyes leaden in the dying light. Lizzie knew that if he chose to stop her there was nothing she would be able to do about it—except, perhaps, scream, and she didn't think that would bother him over-much. But she refused to buckle under his relentless gaze and, with an oddly gracious gesture, he stepped aside and allowed her to pass.

She let out a long breath that she was hardly aware she had been holding, but she firmly resisted the temptation to take to her heels and run back to the house. She walked as slowly as her pounding heart would permit, conscious that his eyes were on her every inch of the way. As she let herself into the house she glanced back, and he was standing quite still where she had left him. It was over. She had called his bluff and he had let her go.

Her bag was lying on the hall table where she had left it when she'd answered the phone. Now, determined not to run, not to panic, she opened it, took out her address book and flipped through it until she found the number she was looking for. She punched it into the telephone; it seemed to take for ever before the connection was finally made, but eventually the number began to ring and was quickly answered. She almost shook with relief, leaning against the table as she was swept by a weakness that betrayed the extent of the tension she was under.

'Sarah,' she said quickly, interrupting the automatic response of her friend's name and number. 'It's Lizzie. I'm in London and I need a bed for the night...' But the voice on the other end continued relentlessly with its message.

Lizzie frowned. It was a moment before she realised that she was talking to an answering machine. She replaced the receiver slowly. It didn't matter, she told herself. She would stay at a hotel. But suddenly she was less confident and, clutching the little book in her hand, she ran up the stairs two at a time.

Angry with herself, she took her time gathering things for her overnight bag, packing neatly. She was a grown woman, not a child to be frightened by the big, bad wolf. There was no way that Noah Jordan could force her to stay in his house. No way he could force her to marry him. She paused briefly as she negotiated the curve of the staircase and saw him in the hall.

He had been using the telephone, and as he saw her he replaced the receiver and watched while she descended the last few steps very slowly, unwilling to confront him. But he made no move to stop her and, gathering her courage, she swept past him without a word.

'Elizabeth.'

She gripped the doorhandle and immediately felt safer. 'What is it?'

'I thought you might need your handbag,' he said, and held it out to her. She would have liked to consign it to hell, and him with it, but he was right. She wouldn't get very far without cash or her credit card.

Reluctantly she relinquished the safety of the door and walked towards him, ready for flight should it prove necessary. However, he made no move to detain her. He released the bag into her care and then crossed the hall to open the front door for her.

'You're letting me go?' she asked, somehow not quite believing it.

'You'll find you're on a very short leash, Elizabeth. I've put a note with my number in your bag. Call me when you need me.'

'Don't hold your breath,' she snapped.

He smiled slightly. 'When you come back we'll discuss the arrangements for the wedding.' And before she realised what was happening she was on the street, the door closed behind her. In a sudden panic she checked for her purse. It was still there. He had seemed so confident that for a moment she thought that he might have taken it, or her credit card, but everything was intact. With a sigh of relief she walked to the corner and hailed a passing taxi.

The hotel Lizzie chose was large, overflowing with tourists—the sort of place she could be anonymous. The clerk at the reception desk was courteous and helpful. 'How will you be paying, Miss French?'

'By credit card.' At his request she handed it over for verification and he ran it through his machine.

'There's a slight delay on the line.' He gave her a professional smile. 'If you don't mind waiting for a moment?' He turned to deal with a query from a lady standing beside her and then retreated into the office.

'Excuse me, miss, I wonder if you would mind stepping this way?' The man at her elbow had eased her away from the desk, and Lizzie frowned as she realised that he was holding her credit card.

'Is something wrong? I haven't spent over my limit, have I?' she said, with a nervous attempt at humour. She had never overspent her limit in her life.

'I'm sure it's nothing we can't sort out,' the man said firmly, 'in a little more privacy.' He steered her to a small office tucked away from the reception area, away from the interested glances they were already beginning to attract.

'Please sit down.' He was polite enough, but it had been an order. 'I have to tell you,' he said once she had complied, 'that this credit card has been reported stolen. It is company policy under the circumstances to call the police. They will be here shortly.'

'Stolen? But that's ridiculous,' she said. 'Why on earth would it have...' she faltered '...been reported stolen?' *Noah*! So this was what he had meant by a short leash.

Noah collected her from the police station two hours later. He had arrived with a senior police officer with whom he was on first-name terms and had vouched for the fact that she was indeed Elizabeth Mary French, and that his report that the credit card had been stolen had been the result of the most unfortunate misunderstanding.

The alternatives had not been attractive. She could have summoned her father from his honeymoon and put him through the unendurable embarrassment of having to bail her out. Or suffered a night in detention. It had been a close decision. It would almost have been worth a night in the police cells to call Noah's bluff and let him try to justify himself to her father.

Two things had stopped her—the fact that the newspapers, already interested because of his marriage to Olivia, would have had a field-day at her father's expense, and also because, never rational when angry, he would almost certainly have believed that she had provoked the entire incident simply to embarrass Olivia.

She glanced across at Noah, his profile a black silhouette against the lighter summer-night sky. He had not uttered one word of apology for what he had put her through. Being escorted from the hotel and driven away in a police car. Having to surrender all her possessions, her belt, the laces of her shoes. The sheer bewilderment of insisting that she was Lizzie French and not being believed. And lastly, and almost the worst of it, as she had signed for her belongings, checking them at the sergeant's insistence against an itemised list, there had been knowing looks from the policemen, who clearly believed that it had been the result of a lover's tiff that had been taken a little too far and thought it was funny.

Surprisingly Noah had made no conditions for her release, doubtless assuming that it would be unnecessary. He had quite ruthlessly demonstrated that he was prepared to go to any lengths to achieve his end. The fact that she had called him instead of her father was clearly acknowledgement enough, as far as he was concerned, that he had won.

She was almost tempted to let him get away with it. After all, she hadn't any other more pressing plans for her life. Having Noah Jordan as a husband would make her the envy of every woman she met. He was a catch by any standard she cared to use. He had money, influence and the kind of sexual magnetism that attracted women like iron filings. And, as his wife, she would be in an excellent position to make quite certain that he paid for those two hours when she had been locked up and treated like a common criminal.

But it wouldn't do. Marriage was a lifetime commitment. Not a weapon to be used for revenge. Noah

Jordan would never know just how fortunate he was that she wasn't the kind of woman he thought her.

'Go and have a shower, Elizabeth,' he instructed as he closed the door behind her. 'You reek of disinfectant.'

'I've had two hours of it; why shouldn't you suffer a little?' she demanded.

'I'll find out the brand they use and you can inflict it on me later if you insist, but we're expecting a visitor in twenty minutes. By then I want you wearing a dress and smelling of something more appropriate than Eau de Nick.'

'Appropriate?' Her forehead buckled in a frown. 'For what?' she asked, turning at the foot of the stairs.

'For the blushing bride-to-be to choose an engagement ring.'

'Woolworth's are doing house calls now?'

'That's not very funny,' he snapped, with uncharacteristic loss of composure.

'I thought it was pretty good under the circumstances. And since you appear to be intent on a fake wedding there isn't much point in wasting good money—'

'The wedding will be real enough, Elizabeth, and so will the ring.'

'It's everything else that will be fake—fake vows, fake smiles, fake kisses... And then what?'

'We'll discuss the details later,' he said dismissively, and turned away.

She came back down the stairs and caught his arm. 'No, we'll discuss them now. I want to know what you're getting out of this.'

For a moment he stared down at her. It was a disconcerting inspection, and she withdrew her hand from his sleeve as if stung. Then he shrugged. '"It is a truth universally acknowledged, that a single man in possession of a good fortune, must be in want of a wife." Or so Olivia never tires of telling me.'

'Horsefeathers!'

He regarded her with disquieting detachment. 'Not entirely. And you will at least keep a number of hopeful aspirants at bay.'

'I don't believe I'm hearing this...'

'Please don't make the mistake of thinking that I am not entirely serious.'

No. She wouldn't do that, she thought. He was clearly in the most deadly earnest. 'Wouldn't it make it simpler if love was part of the equation?' she asked, a little hoarsely.

'Love...?' He laid his hand against her cheek. 'You want love?'

'No.' She took a step back, but the newel post blocked her retreat, and suddenly he was far too close.

'That's easy.' And he proceeded to demonstrate just how easy it was as the simple touch of his lips to her neck brought a gasp choking from her throat.

'Please, Noah.'

He raised his head briefly. 'You see?' But he clearly didn't expect an answer because he was already kissing her—tender, delicate, pleasing little kisses that offered no threat. Not until she realised that she was responding in kind, encouraging him, her arms about his neck, moaning softly as he pulled away. 'You do see, Elizabeth? Love is just a pretty word to dignify our lusts. A straightforward business arrangement will do me just fine. And if it keeps you out of Francesca's hair so much the better.'

She wanted to strike him, scratch his eyes out. Instead she turned and ran up the stairs, flinging off clothes that reeked of the police station and Noah Jordan. Standing under a steaming shower, she washed the taste of him away, the imprint of his hands. And all the time Francesca Hallam's name beat a constant tattoo inside her head.

She was behind all this. What was it about that woman that so absorbed him? Right from the first moment they had met at the wedding he had seemed drawn to her, inviting her to join them that evening when surely the best thing would have been to keep them apart. She would have sworn that they had never met before, and yet...

She would have stayed in her room, locked the door, but she knew there was no point. He would break it down if necessary. She would play this one last game...

Fifteen minutes later she descended to the drawing room, wearing an ivory silk shirt over a pair of soft crêpe trousers in a rich claret. She hadn't had time to wash her hair, but she was enveloped in an invisible cloud of L'Air du Temps that Peter had bought her from the duty-free when he'd come home last Christmas. It was a very small, ironical gesture that no one would ever know about. But nevertheless, it helped to lift her mouth into a warm smile.

Tomorrow, however, was another day. Tomorrow she would leave his house and never look back.

He was talking to a tiny, grey-haired man, and they both turned and stood up as she entered the drawing room. Noah immediately came towards her, taking both her hands in his, his features arranged in a fair approximation of a smile. 'There you are, darling.' He put his arm around her shoulder and drew her over to the sofa to introduce her to the jeweller, who wasted no time in opening a case lined with black velvet to show off the glittering treasure it contained.

'Diamonds and sapphires, Noah, as you suggested.' He smiled as Lizzie drew in a sharp breath. 'You were right, of course. With the colour of the young lady's eyes...it has to be a blue stone.'

Noah, who had taken up a position behind the sofa, made a gesture at the tray. 'So, my darling,' he said, 'which one will it be?'

Lizzie winced at the 'darling', and her eyes swept the tray for something to make him smart a little in return. It wasn't difficult. An exquisite deep blue rectangular sapphire flanked by smaller, similarly cut diamonds stood out a mile. It had to be the most expensive ring on the tray, and although she had no intention of keeping it, of ever wearing it, Noah wasn't to know that.

For a while she ignored the ring, trying on one or two of the smaller stones and lifting her hand for Noah's inspection, teasing him a little. 'It's difficult,' she sighed. 'They are all so beautiful.'

Noah reached over her shoulder. 'This one,' he said, and picked up the ring she had intended from the first. He took her left hand in his and slipped it onto her finger. For just a moment their eyes met, and with the slightest lift of dark, expressive brows he indicated that he knew precisely what she had been doing and wasn't in the least bit impressed.

Her eyes dropped quickly to the ring. It was a perfect fit, and the blue stone seemed to leap into life against her skin as she held out her hand to admire it. He turned to the jeweller without waiting for her agreement. 'Did you bring wedding rings, Marcus?'

After the jeweller had gone the house seemed very quiet. 'Drink?' Noah asked, pouring himself a whisky.

'A gin and tonic, please. Plenty of tonic.'

He handed her the glass. 'I've spoken to your father, Elizabeth, and told him about the wedding.'

'Already?' she asked, dismayed that he should ever have to learn of this nonsense.

'I didn't want there to be any mistake.'

She refused to look at him. It was a complication, but once she had extricated herself from Noah's clutches she would write and explain. 'What did you say to him?'

'I indicated that the wedding was...a formality.'

'A formality?' Lizzie asked, puzzled, then understanding brought a scarlet blush to her cheeks. 'How could you? How could you do that?' she demanded.

'With the greatest of difficulty, I can assure you. Telling him that I had been unable to help myself, that I had fallen hopelessly in love with you the moment I first set eyes on you, that I had overborne all your objections and, since we had used no protection, speed was—'

'Oh, God.' She covered her mouth with her hand.

'Quite. The words nearly stuck in my throat.'

'What...what did he say?'

'He appeared somewhat stunned—'

'Are you surprised?' she demanded. 'I hardly know you.'

He shrugged. 'Fathers are notoriously one-eyed about their daughter's...desires. However, he gathered his wits sufficiently to tell me at length how fortunate I am. You are apparently blessed with every quality a man could wish for in a wife.' He shrugged. 'He and Olivia are going to bless us with their presence at the wedding, by the way, so it will be fourteen for dinner on Thursday. Or perhaps you would like to invite a few more of your own friends?'

'No, thank you. And after dinner? When the guests have gone—what then?'

He regarded her steadily. 'I shan't trouble you—'

She made an impatient gesture. He had made his distaste for her more than plain. She was no classic beauty, no competition for the kind of women he was usually seen with, she knew, although why he found her quite so repulsive... It would be a victory of sorts to make him desire her.

She caught herself as Noah's eyes narrowed, wondering if her thoughts had somehow been betrayed in her expression. It all was academic anyway. She had no intention of going through with this marriage, but he would expect her to show some interest, would become suspicious if she didn't.

'I didn't mean that,' she said. What had she meant? She took a sip of her drink; she needed a little time... 'It will be two years before we can get a quiet, tidy divorce with no questions asked,' she said, with a sudden flash of inspiration. 'I'm sure you don't intend to live like a monk in all that time.'

'Are you offering your services, Elizabeth?' He was pouring himself another drink, and when she didn't answer he turned around.

'No,' she said quickly.

'How pleasant to have found something about which we are in complete agreement.' He stretched out in a wing-chair in front of the fireplace, his legs crossed carelessly, his head thrown back against the old blue brocade. 'However, your estimate is a little short of the mark.'

'Estimate?'

'Two years. It will take a little longer than that, I'm afraid. It would raise a few eyebrows if we parted a few days after the wedding.'

So. She had guessed right. 'How much longer?' she asked, with every appearance of interest.

'Six months.'

'Do you think we could stand one another that long?'

'If I can put up with you, I don't see why you should find it so very difficult. You won't lack any comfort, and I have no doubt you'll make the most of it.'

It was impossible to miss the little barb buried in his words, and the beautiful sapphire seemed suddenly to weigh a ton upon her finger. 'And then what?'

He sipped his drink, deep in thought. 'I'll think of something. Perhaps you'll arrive at a party one evening to find I'm already there with another woman. We'll have a very public row and that will be the end of one more marriage.' He raised his glass in mock salute. 'Nothing very remarkable. I've seen it happen half a dozen times.'

'Then you keep extremely bad company.' Lizzie stood up. 'I'm going to bed.'

'Before you go...'

She turned in the doorway. 'What is it?'

'It's rather a long time since lunch. I thought you might care to demonstrate your wifely virtues and make some supper.' He was goading her quite deliberately.

'I was given a cup of tea and a sandwich at the police station.' Not that she had eaten it. 'And, since I'm not your wife *yet*, Noah Jordan—' nor ever would be '—you can make your own damned supper.'

Lizzie lay in the unaccustomed luxury of the lace-draped double bed of Noah's guest suite and tried to work out her best plan of escape. Her first—to leave as soon as she was sure that Noah was asleep—had to be abandoned because of the extensive burglar-alarm system. Once it was switched on any movement downstairs would set it off. She wouldn't be able to leave unnoticed until Mrs Harper came in, probably around seven o'clock.

Then what? She wouldn't have a credit card until the bank replaced the one that had been 'stolen' and can-

celled. She had a little over twenty pounds in her purse.
She could get another fifty from the cash-card machine.
Or had Noah cancelled that card too? Well, Sarah would
be back in the morning—she had work to go to—and
she would be able to cash a cheque for her. Lizzie let
out a slightly shaky sigh of relief and went to sleep.

She was already dressed when a tap on the door announced Mrs Harper.

'Miss Lizzie? Goodness, you are up early.'

'I'm always up by seven, Mrs Harper. What can I do
for you?'

'Oh, it's this.' She held out an envelope. 'I found it
in the letterbox this morning. Someone must have delivered it personally some time during the night.'

Lizzie took the envelope, immediately recognising
Peter's handwriting. 'Did Mr Jordan see this?' she asked.

'No, dear. I was just on my way to take him his tea.'

'Don't mention it, will you? It's a surprise I'm ar-
ranging for him . . .' Oh, how glibly the lie rolled from
her tongue. It was hateful.

But Mrs Harper was smiling. 'Mr Jordan told me your
good news last night. I popped across when I saw the
light on in the kitchen . . . We live in the mews at the
back there.' She beamed. 'I hope you'll be very happy.'

Lizzie's embarrassment was acute. 'Thank you, Mrs
Harper.'

'And I won't say a word about the letter,' she reassured her as she turned to leave.

Lizzie gripped the envelope for a moment, her first
instinct to destroy it unopened. He must have been crazy,
she thought, creeping about in the night to deliver letters.
It could just as easily have been Noah who had taken it
from the letterbox. She stared at the envelope. Just how
crazy had he been? In a sudden panic she tore it open.

Lizzie,

I've been lying awake half the night trying to make sense of everything and I think I understand. You're just trying to make me think you don't care and you've persuaded Jordan to play along with you. You had me fooled for a moment, but I know you too well. It's all a sham. Just like my marriage. I owe her nothing, Lizzie. I love you, I always have. You know that. I'll be waiting for you at Sloane Square station. Come as soon as you can. I'm never going back. Peter.

Lizzie looked at her overnight bag and abandoned it without a second thought. Convincing Peter that he was wrong was more important than escape. She had three days to get away. All the time in the world.

As she passed Noah's bedroom Lizzie heard him moving about. The sounds lent wings to her heels and she flew swiftly and silently down the long staircase and let herself out of the house.

The road was almost deserted; there was not even a cruising taxi to lend her speed. She almost ran to the corner, but once out of sight slowed a little, desperately trying to think what she could say to a man who was clearly coming apart at the seams. How she could convince him that he must stay with his wife and forget all about her.

He didn't believe that she was Noah's lover. She pulled a face. If Noah had assumed a little less about her relationship with Peter, he might have anticipated that, she thought. It didn't suit Peter's vanity to believe that she would leap into bed with a man she barely knew. Not when she had held him at bay for so long. She stopped. Why had she? She shook her head. It no longer mattered.

Sloane Square loomed up all too quickly. Peter was standing by the entrance to the underground station, looking anxiously at his watch, when she saw him. He glanced up, saw her, hurried forward to clasp her hands. 'Lizzie. I knew you'd come.'

'I had to, Peter.'

'I know. I know you love me. How can I have ever been so stupid? Lizzie, darling, can you ever forgive me?'

The boyish grin was like a knife going through her. Two days ago—only two—those words would have made her the happiest girl alive. Now they made her feel quite sick. She withdrew her hands from his grasp. 'Is there somewhere we can sit down, Peter? We have to talk.'

'There's a little place around the corner,' he said, missing her lack of enthusiasm in his own eagerness.

He fetched two coffees from the counter and sat opposite her. 'Oh, Lizzie. My little—'

'Peter, there's something I have to tell you,' she said quickly, to stop him. It was odd how she had once thought the way he called her 'little' Lizzie endearing. Now she found it simply patronising. What kind of fool did he take her for? Did he really think that she would ignore the fact that he was married to someone else?

Why on earth had she never seen him this clearly before? Never seen the underlying weakness in his character? Because like everyone else she had never looked too closely beneath the surface. Good-looking, clever, he had always been able to get his own way. He had always been spoilt—by his family, his teachers. They had enjoyed indulging him.

And girls. Had they enjoyed indulging him too? Whilst there had been no evidence of his infidelities she had been able to pretend that they did not exist. But now she knew. He had never pressed her to sleep with him. If her father had not been so ill, if she had managed to get away, go to Florence or Paris with him when he had asked her, it would have happened, she knew that. But at home, under her father's eyes, he had been circumspect—too circumspect for a healthy young male.

It was as if a veil had been lifted from her eyes. Maybe he had loved her a little, but she was certain that Peter Hallam hadn't loved her enough to remain celibate through all those years.

His thoughts seemed to be running along similar lines. 'I am right, Lizzie. I know I am right. You're not sleeping with Jordan.' He laughed. 'I mean, I should know. You're so puritanical—'

She had never thought of herself as puritanical. Just sensible. 'I'm afraid you're wrong, Peter. That Lizzie doesn't exist any more. And you are married.'

Peter's fair skin flushed angrily. 'She caught me on the rebound, Lizzie. When you let me down—'

'I didn't let you down, Peter.' Lizzie's eyes glittered like the sapphire tucked deep into her pocket. She stretched her fingers out to touch it. 'I imagine you've been bouncing from bed to bed all your adult life. I'm just unfinished business—the one that got away—'

'No! You weren't like all those other girls, Lizzie. You were *different—special*.'

She was sure that he meant it—maybe he actually believed it—but she couldn't afford to weaken. 'No. Just unavailable,' she said, a little unkindly. She looked him straight in the eye. 'And you couldn't wait—'

'Wait? That's all you could ever say,' he said, angry now. 'No explanation, just "wait".'

'I told you, Dad needed me.'

'If you had left he would have pulled himself together. I needed you, Lizzie...'

'Not any more. You have Francesca,' she reminded him.

He pulled a face. 'She told me she was having my child,' he said bitterly.

'She miscarried, Peter.' She felt enormous pity for them both. 'It happens sometimes. There'll be other babies.' Lizzie understood that he felt somehow betrayed; if he knew that Fran was pregnant again he wouldn't be pleading with her to go away with him like this.

Tempting as it was to tell him, she knew she couldn't. She could understand Fran's reluctance to say anything too soon. She must have all the time she needed. And it was in her, Lizzie's, power to give her that time. And because in some part this nightmare was her fault, because she had given up Peter for her father and then thought that she could call him back when it suited her, she must make it right.

'You shouldn't have come back, Peter.'

'You invited me. Or was that before you set your stall out for Noah Jordan?' He gave a hollow laugh. 'Be realistic, Lizzie. What on earth could you offer a man like that? He's had affairs with some of the most beautiful women . . .'

She ignored the implied insult, holding for one moment longer the sapphire engagement ring that she had brought with her—a last resort that she had prayed she wouldn't have to use. Now she slipped the ring onto her finger. 'Then it's very flattering that he chose to marry me.'

'Marry you?' His laughter was very cruel.

'Noah asked me to marry him yesterday.' He stared at her, the smile wiped from his face as she held out her left hand.

He grasped her fingers, staring at the ring for many seconds. Finally he raised his head. 'Why?'

Lizzie swallowed. 'I'm such a perfect home body, of course. Not much use for anything else...'

Peter dropped her hand and sat back. 'So that's it. The man wants an untainted virgin to breed from.' Lizzie was beginning to feel sick. 'He won't be faithful to you—you know that, don't you?'

'And you would be?' she demanded. 'Your track record isn't very convincing, and you've only been married two months.' Peter had the grace to look discomfited, but it was time to do what she had come for, even if it meant lying through her teeth. She lifted her shoulders in a tiny shrug. 'Noah may not be perfect husband material, Peter, but then who is? And he can give me everything I want.'

'You're marrying him because he's rich?' Peter went almost grey as the colour deserted his face.

She had finally managed to shock him, get him to listen. Now was the moment. She dwelt for a moment on the memory of the way Noah had kissed her in the theatre. How his lips had teased hers apart, the taste of him. And in the garden, when she had fought him, the scent of his skin, his thighs pressed against hers. She gave a little shiver. 'Not just because he's rich, Peter,' she said, from somewhere deep in her throat.

Peter leapt to his feet. 'My God, you're almost trembling just thinking about him.' She didn't answer, but it wasn't, she was shocked to discover, too far from the truth. 'But you said you loved me.' Peter's petulant voice dragged her back to the tiny café.

'Love?' She appeared to consider the concept for a moment and then shrugged. 'I imagine you told Fran you loved her when you took her to bed.' From somewhere she managed a smile. 'Love can be a very transient thing, Peter. Marriage is for ever.'

'Lizzie...?' He was utterly bewildered. She rose a little shakily to her feet, picked up her bag. 'No,' he said, a little desperately, 'I don't believe you. None of this is true. You just want to hurt me.'

'Why should I hurt you, Peter? You seem to be making a pretty good job of that yourself. Go back to your wife and remember why you married her.' She turned in the doorway. 'Oh, by the way, the wedding is to take place some time on Thursday. Noah suggested that you and Francesca might like to be witnesses.'

CHAPTER SIX

LIZZIE didn't wait for Peter's reaction. 'Don't mention it to Fran. I expect Noah will give her a ring later, at your hotel in Stratford.' She moved swiftly back to him and put her hands on his shoulders, brushing his cheek with her lips. 'Goodbye, Peter. Give my love to Fran.' And she left him standing over the two cooling cups of coffee, hurrying away before he could see the brightness of threatened tears in her eyes.

Noah, elegantly dressed for business in a dark grey suit and striped shirt, stood up as she entered the breakfast room twenty minutes later. If he noticed that she was pale... Well, under the circumstances it was hardly surprising. But he said nothing about her pallor. He said nothing at all.

'Good morning, Noah.' Her voice, at any rate, was steady enough.

He seemed to remember himself and pulled out a chair for her. 'Elizabeth. Did you sleep well?'

'Well enough.' Her hand barely shook as she poured herself some coffee, she noted absently, which was odd, considering her insides were like jelly. 'You'd better tell me what we are doing today,' she continued with every evidence of outward calm. 'What time are we going to see the registrar to make the wedding arrangements?'

'You haven't changed your mind, then?'

The inflexion in his voice warned her that there was more behind his query than simple curiosity. She turned to meet his measuring gaze. 'I wasn't aware that I had the option.'

'You haven't. But I looked in on you a little while ago. Your bags are packed and you were ... missing.'

She hadn't anticipated that. 'It wasn't another escape attempt, Noah. I've learned my lesson. I just went out for some air.'

'The garden was too stuffy for you?' he enquired, with the urbane air of someone who might easily be persuaded that this was the case, but she was not fooled. Not for a minute.

'I wanted to walk, Noah,' she said a little desperately. 'I walk every morning.'

Through the woods, down to the lake to feed the ducks—it was a routine, something she had started to get her father out of bed, out of his chair, out of the house. She had invented improbable stories of fox attacks, pondweed invasions, the sighting of some rare bird—anything to spark him into life, even if it was only to irritation at her apparent stupidity. More recently it had become a joke. He had begun to press her to wilder inventions, making a game of it.

She swallowed hard. So much time and effort was about to be destroyed by one selfish woman. Perhaps she should offer the Fates her own small sacrifice to placate them. Back in control, she raised her eyes to meet his. 'Walking doesn't need a credit card, Noah. What did you want this morning? Or were you simply checking up on me?'

For a moment his eyes sparked. 'I was—' His jaw muscles tightened as he bit down hard on his anger. 'I was simply checking up on you. With good reason it seems.' He produced an envelope from his pocket. 'I found this.' He handed it to her. 'That, presumably, is Peter Hallam's handwriting?'

She stared at the envelope. How on earth could she have been so careless? She had tucked the letter safely away in her handbag. 'Yes. He wanted me to meet him.'

'Why? What did you threaten him with?'

Her brows drew together in a frown. '"Threaten"? What on earth do you mean?'

'It can't have been easy for him to get away. He would hardly have taken such a risk willingly.'

Lizzie's mind was racing at top speed. It had been difficult enough to convince Peter that she had dumped him for a rich husband—he knew her too well. But if Noah discovered that it was Peter doing the chasing, that she was the innocent party, he might decide that he didn't need to marry her after all. For Fran and her baby she wasn't prepared to take the risk.

She crossed her fingers behind her back. Getting married had been Noah's bright idea, although she was no nearer to working out his motive. It no longer mattered. Whatever it was, she didn't feel the least bit guilty about hijacking it for her own reasons.

'He still loves me,' she said, with every appearance of mutiny, defying him with her eyes. 'I know he does.'

Noah erupted from his seat and dragged her to her feet, his fingers biting into her arm. 'How can such a lovely face hide such selfishness?' She flinched from fierce, ransacking eyes, appalled at the reaction she had provoked. 'When I first saw you, I thought—' He stopped, apparently to gather himself before he said something that they would both regret, but she wasn't about to let him off that hook.

'Just what *did* you think, Noah? Why don't you tell me and put us both out of our misery?'

He took a deep breath. 'What I thought doesn't matter one bit. And, to answer your earlier question, we'll be seeing the registrar some time this morning. I'll phone you when I've arranged a time, so if the urge for fresh air overcomes you again resist it. No more little walks, Elizabeth.'

'I've more than enough to keep me occupied here organising dinner with Mrs Harper for our guests on Thursday.' She pulled ineffectually at her arm, regarding him with loathing. 'Would you like me to organise a three-tier wedding cake while I'm at it?'

'Why stop at three? You can have as many damned tiers as the fancy takes you.' Then he yanked her close and kissed her hard upon the mouth before finally releasing her. 'I'll see you later,' he said a little gruffly.

For a moment she was stunned into silence. Then as he straightened she saw that Mrs Harper had come into the room. The kiss had been for her benefit.

'I can't wait,' she murmured, the forced smile trembling on her lips.

Did Noah really believe that a kiss over the breakfast table would convince Mrs Harper that they were love's young dream? If they had been living in a small house without staff it would have been possible to keep up the pretence for the outside world, but they would never be able to hide the true state of their marriage from the housekeeper. She crumpled back onto her chair as the full impact of what she had done began to sink in.

'What are you going to do with yourself for the rest of the day?' Noah asked a little stiffly after they had visited the registrar to make the arrangements for their wedding. He was being very formal, very civilised. Numbingly so. Was that what she had condemned herself to for the next six months? she wondered miserably. She almost preferred the insults, the rows. At least when she was fighting with Noah she felt alive.

'I thought I'd shop for my trousseau.' She chose to be deliberately provoking.

He refused to be provoked, opening the car door for her without the slightest change in his expression. 'In that case I'd better organise some money for you, since your credit card has been cancelled.'

'There's no need. I've already organised a replacement. I'm picking it up from the Piccadilly branch of my bank this morning.' He raised his brows in somewhat sardonic admiration of her efficiency. 'In view of last night's little fiasco, they were terribly keen to be as helpful as possible,' she explained.

'And no doubt you gave them the strong impression that you might take your business elsewhere if they weren't?'

'I didn't have to threaten them, Noah. I simply explained that as I was getting married this week I would be needing to use it rather... enthusiastically.'

He half smiled. 'So, you're not just a pretty face.'

'Not even a pretty face, surely?'

'The face, Elizabeth, is quite extraordinarily beautiful,' he said, so intently that it brought a blush flooding to her cheeks. 'Unfortunately in your case the beauty is only skin-deep.'

The silence that followed this remark could have been cut with a knife.

As they reached the gallery Noah turned to her. 'Keep the car for the rest of the day; Harper will look after you. Olivia uses him all the time, so he's bound to know just where to take you shopping. You can pick me up at about four.'

'Perhaps I'll just ask him to take me to Stratford for a little sightseeing,' she replied stonily.

His face tightened. 'You could try it. He would, of course, check with me first. Four o'clock.'

'Noah?' she called as he strode across the pavement towards the gallery.

He turned. 'What is it?'

'I was wondering,' she asked a little huskily, well aware that Harper was listening to every word, 'what kind of nightgowns you prefer? Black lace? Slinky satin? Or perhaps you'd consider scarlet more appropriate?'

'Don't bother for me, darling,' he drawled. 'I never wear the things.' And his chilling smile warned her that any attempt to embarrass him would be a two-edged weapon.

Harper was indeed a mine of information. Lizzie joined him in the front of the car, and after a discussion with him, and with the help of the car phone, her first port of call was a hair salon where a diminutive cockney used a pair of scissors with lightning efficiency to strip away hair by the yard.

'There you are, duchess,' he said eventually, with a soft chuckle. 'What d'you think?' Tentatively she raised her hand to her hair. Shoulder-length, her hair bounced into a curve she had never suspected it capable of, the skilled cutting giving it a fullness that her own efforts at styling had never achieved. 'Well?' he prompted.

Lizzie swallowed, hardly able to believe that such a transformation was possible. Then a slow smile spread across her face. 'I love it. Thank you.'

When she emerged from the salon Harper was waiting to take her to her next appointment. A facial and a lesson in cosmetic art followed, then it was on to a series of boutiques.

She emerged from the last with her voile print dress folded in a bag, and wearing instead a pair of wide trousers with a matching cardigan jacket in a soft cream crêpe de Chine over a loose roll-neck silk overblouse, the colour of very dry sherry to echo the lights in her hair.

She checked her watch. It was three-thirty—too late for any more shopping—so she asked Harper to drive straight to the gallery. The receptionist, a rather superior blonde, came forward. 'Can I help you, madam?'

'Is Mr Jordan about?' she asked.

It gave Lizzie considerable pleasure to realise that the girl was unable to decide whether Lizzie was a possible client or one of Noah's girlfriends. Until today, she thought, suppressing a desperate desire to giggle, she wouldn't have considered either option a possibility. 'He's engaged at the moment,' she said carefully. 'Would you care to wait until he's free, or can I make an appointment for you?'

'There's no need. He asked me to pick him up at four.'

'Oh, right.' The girl relaxed and smiled more easily. 'I'll let him know you're here.' She reached for a phone.

'No, don't disturb him. I'm early. I'll just look around for a while, if I won't be in the way.'

'Well, I'm afraid the upstairs gallery is closed this week—it's being rehung for an exhibition—but help yourself to the ground floor. Would you like some coffee while you're waiting?'

Lizzie declined, and moved into the ground-floor gallery space. It was white—totally white—and the paintings stood out like exclamation points—vivid, brilliant slashes of colour and texture. Lizzie became totally absorbed as she moved from canvas to canvas.

'You seem fascinated by that painting. Can I tell you about the artist? We've more of his work downstairs, if you'd care to see it.' She had heard him come down the open-tread stairs, promise his companion that he would have lunch with him soon, then excuse himself, crossing the dark polished oak floor towards her, and she assumed that he had noticed her waiting for him.

'Do you invite all the young women who come into your gallery down to the basement, Noah?' She turned, smiling a little to tease him for not recognising her. 'I warn you that it will have to stop—' But the shock that widened his eyes, darkened the skin across his cheekbones, brought her to a halt.

'Stop?' His searching glance took in every detail of her appearance, but the shutters were down now; she would have missed that first raw, exposed moment of stunned surprise if she hadn't had the advantage of him.

'When we're married,' she finished. She tried to maintain the light, teasing tone, but her voice shook too much.

'You expect me to be faithful, then?'

'Oh, I'm afraid I shall have to insist on it,' she said, with an attempt at a sophisticated laugh. Under Noah's probing eyes it was little more than a croak. 'I'm sure you'll expect no less of me,' she added somewhat lamely.

'While you live with me as my wife, I too shall expect total fidelity,' he confirmed, then, seizing her wrist, he led her to a door which he flung open.

'Where are we going?'

'To the basement, my dear. Since we have a few minutes to spare, I want you to see exactly what happens when I take anyone down there. No matter how young and pretty.'

Stairs led down through the workroom, where a couple of men were crating up some pictures. They glanced up, nodded and then continued with their work.

'A few minutes to spare before what?' she enquired, anxious to change the subject.

'Before our appointment with my solicitor.' He saw concern pucker her brow. 'Just a few formalities.

Nothing to worry about.' He switched on a bank of lights and flooded the cool underground area with light. 'Now, as you can see,' he began sarcastically, 'no bed, no sofa. Only a couple of gilt chairs for the creakier of my clients. Nothing, in fact, conducive to seduction.'

But Lizzie had forgotten all about her teasing. She gazed in wonder at the long racks. 'But there are hundreds of pictures here.'

'Quite a lot,' he agreed. 'Not all the business is done upstairs.' Sensing that she was genuinely interested, he pulled out a canvas. 'What do you think of this? The artist is young, but he's been bringing me his paintings since I saw some of his work at a college exhibition. He's beginning to make a name for himself. Next year I'll give him an exhibition. Then there'll be a waiting list for his work.'

'You have that much power?'

Noah didn't reply.

'Is this one of his?'

'You like it?'

'It's beautiful.'

'Yes. I'm very tempted to buy it myself, before he gets too expensive. You've a good eye for a picture,' he said as he slid it back into place. 'Have you ever been to an auction?'

'Only a charity thing at the village fête,' she said as she walked along the racks, enjoying the tantalising glimpses of vivid colour, the scent of fresh oil-paint. 'I bought a picture of a pig, for five pounds.'

'A pig?' His brows drew together in concentration. 'Surely you don't mean the one in the hall at Dove Court?'

'Yes, that's the one.' She laughed. 'You've obviously seen it. Dad thinks it's awful, but I just...' Noah was shaking his head in disbelief. 'What?'

'If you ever decide to sell it, let me know.'

'Sell it? Why would I...? Good Lord, are you telling me that it's valuable?'

'On a good day at auction?' He considered. 'It should fetch upwards of five thousand pounds.'

'Five thousand...? But it's not even insured!' Then her initial excitement was dampened. 'Damn. I really love that pig.'

'I'll arrange cover for you if you like,' Noah offered.

'Would you? It'll only be temporary, until I can sell it.'

'You love it *that* much?' he remarked cuttingly. 'I suppose I shouldn't be surprised. It's always the ones who declare they would never part with a painting at any price who dash to the salerooms when they scent real money.'

His contempt was only equalled by her anger. 'Then I am more than happy to live down to your expectations, Noah. But, since you're so disapproving, I won't trouble you with the details of the sale. I'll ask Dad to send it to one of the big auction houses.'

'Oh, no, you don't. I'll handle it. We don't want people to think you don't trust me. That would be very bad for business.' Then he shrugged. 'Besides, I've a couple of clients who might be interested. I'm sure you have no objection to getting the best possible price for the picture?'

'On the contrary,' she declared furiously. 'The higher the better. How soon can it be sent to auction?'

'Leave it with me. In the meantime, perhaps you'd like to go to a sale to see how it's done,' he offered as they made their way back up the stairs.

'I'd enjoy that. When can we go?'

'One afternoon next week, if you like—'

'You forget, I intend to have a job by next week. We still have a bet and, since I'll be staying with you rather longer than I had anticipated, it's all the more important that I win.'

'You're not going to have much time for job-hunting. Besides, that was yesterday. Things have changed since then. All bets are off.'

'I see. You expect me to stay at home and be a proper little wife for you?'

'You would prefer to be an improper one?' he offered.

'I would prefer not to be your wife at all, Noah, as well you know,' she said swiftly, but the colour still rose painfully to her cheeks. 'But, if you're defaulting on our bet, I believe I win.'

'I'll take you to see *Aida*,' he promised. 'And any other show you'd like to see. We'll have to do something to pass the time.' He paused. 'But about clothes. You are going to need rather more than a couple of pairs of jeans. I do a lot of entertaining.'

'I do have a dress or two—'

'I know,' he said wryly. 'I've seen them. I've spoken to the bank about a personal account for you. You're to call in tomorrow to provide specimen signatures. Until you get your cheque book just keep any bills and I'll see you're refunded.' His eyes flickered briefly over her new outfit. 'I like that. And your hair. But you don't need quite so much make-up.' Then he glanced at the wafer-thin gold watch on his wrist. 'I think we'd better go,' he said, apparently taking her stunned silence for acquiescence.

He spoke briefly to his receptionist on the way out and then ushered her out to the car. 'I've asked your father to send up your birth certificate, by the way, but when you speak to him about the painting will you ask him to send your passport as well? It'll need changing to your new name. In fact, I think Harper had better go and fetch them tomorrow morning.'

'Why do you want my passport? Have you decided to take me on some glamorous honeymoon?'

He regarded her with something close to amusement. 'Would you like that? A warm, tropical island, perhaps, with days spent under a shady palm, sipping an exotic cocktail through a straw from a coconut? And the nights—'

'Forget the nights.'

'And the nights, dancing under the stars. You know, it's not such a bad idea. I'd really like to take you to a desert island, Elizabeth,' he drawled, very softly so that Harper should not hear. Startled, Lizzie blushed. 'And leave you there, where you couldn't do any harm.'

As a conversation-stopper it was certainly effective. Lizzie withdrew to the far corner of the Bentley and stared out at the passing traffic, her hands screwed into tight little fists until the anger abated. He was insufferable, infuriating.

She told herself that it wasn't entirely his fault. Olivia had told him a pack of lies about her and today she had added her own fuel to fire his derision. But however much she told herself that she didn't care one jot what he thought about her, that it didn't hurt, she was disquieted to find that it did. It was beginning to hurt rather a lot.

She glanced across at him. His head thrown back against the leather upholstery of the car, his eyes closed, he looked less threatening, more approachable. The brief glimpses that she had caught of this more human Noah Jordan were tantalising. Any woman he loved, she found herself thinking, would feel like a queen. But he didn't believe in love. Noah opened his eyes, and for a moment the glance they exchanged was all question.

'What is it?' he demanded. She shook her head help-lessly. She didn't know what it was. Then Harper brought the car to a halt and Noah turned away. 'We're here,' he said abruptly, breaking the spell.

He helped her out of the car, and by the time they were inside she had herself firmly under control. She was able to smile and shake hands with Noah's solicitor as if she was indeed the most happy bride-to-be.

The man settled them in his office, ordered tea and then produced a legal document. 'Shall I explain this for Miss French, Noah?' he asked. 'Or would you prefer to do it?' Noah indicated by a sharp shake of his head that he would prefer nothing of the kind. 'Very well.' And he began to explain.

The document was a pre-marital contract. Lizzie had heard of such things and listened with interest to the clauses about property, discovering that Noah had a country home as well as the London house, both of which would remain with Noah in the event of a breakdown in the marriage. The business was also to remain untouched. The solicitor asked her if she under-stood. She glanced at Noah.

'None of this is necessary,' she said.

Noah said nothing, but the solicitor smiled reassur-ingly. 'I'm sure it's not. It's simply a precaution to protect inherited property. Quite normal, these days. And, of course, your own settlement in the event of divorce would not be insubstantial.' He glanced at the document. 'In the event of a total breakdown of the marriage within the first five years resulting in divorce, and providing there is no issue—'

'Issue?'

'Children,' Noah interjected a little sharply.

'Oh.'

The solicitor waited briefly to see if she had any other query on this point, and she shook her head. He carried on. 'Providing there is no issue, there will be a one-off payment of two hundred and fifty thousand pounds.' After that, he continued to explain, there would be a rising scale of payments.

'And if there is... issue?' Noah turned to stare at her and Lizzie swallowed hard, wondering what on earth had prompted her to ask such a stupid question.

'Separate arrangements will be negotiated at the time,' the solicitor assured her. 'In view of the somewhat hurried nature of your union, Mr Jordan thought it best to leave it until later, when a more considered judgment can be made.' He regarded her thoughtfully. 'However, if you're concerned we can, of course, leave this for another day or two—'

'No. It can wait,' Noah interrupted.

'I think, perhaps, Miss French has the right to decide that,' the solicitor intervened quite gently.

'It doesn't matter,' Lizzie said quickly as the atmosphere grew steadily more tense. 'Noah is right. It will wait.' The point, after all, would never arise. 'Can I look at the document?'

'I've paraphrased it, of course, to make it as simple as I can. Your own solicitor will advise you on any points that are unclear.'

'That won't be necessary.'

The solicitor glanced at Noah, but, receiving no help from that direction, turned back to Lizzie. 'May I assume, then, that you wish to sign now?'

'I should like to read it for myself.'

'Of course,' he said a little indulgently, and handed the agreement to her. And in that quiet room, while the dust motes danced in the slanting rays of the sun, Lizzie read every painful word, slowly and carefully so that she would be sure that she had not misunderstood. Finally she raised her head. 'Is everything clear, Miss French?'

'Quite clear.' It was quite clear that Noah thought that she would try to take him for every penny she could get when it came to their divorce.

Did he really believe that if that had been her intention a mere quarter of a million pounds would have bought her off? Just one of his paintings—the small Picasso that had pride of place in the drawing room, for instance—was worth at least ten times that. Perhaps more.

'Then shall we sign...?' The man smiled, clearly relieved to get the awkward moment over with, and offered her a pen. She didn't take it.

'No, I don't think so. Thank you.' She replaced the document carefully on the desk and then rose to her feet. She offered the solicitor her hand and he took it, somewhat uncertainly. 'Thank you for your patience. I'm sorry you've been put to so much trouble for nothing.'

Then, without sparing Noah Jordan a single glance, she walked from the building and climbed into the Bentley.

'Please take me home, Harper,' she said.

CHAPTER SEVEN

LIZZIE jumped as the door of the morning room snapped shut behind Noah. 'Very clever, Elizabeth.' His voice was soft. Too soft.

Her hand shook a little, and a battalion of butterflies invaded her abdomen as she slowly raised her eyes from the book she was pretending to read. She hardly knew what had driven her, shivering despite the August heat, from that solicitor's office. But she had had the best part of an hour to work it out.

The offhanded assumption that she would need to be bought off, that she had not one whit of honour had been a severe shock. If she had wanted his wretched money she would surely have leapt at the chance of marriage, no matter how loveless an affair it was to have been. That he couldn't see that had cut like a knife-wound to her heart.

And that scared her. Because, as misunderstanding and insult had followed each other with increasing intensity, piling one on another, she had managed somehow to convince herself that she didn't care tuppence what Noah Jordan thought of her. But this final hurt had tumbled the pile about her ears, so that only the rags of pride had stopped her from screaming and tearing the miserable contract to shreds.

It had taken every second of the long hour that had ensued, while she'd waited for his return, to gather herself, to remind herself why she was marrying him. But it had been touch-and-go.

'Clever?' She managed to sound vaguely surprised. She'd known that he would be angry with her, but as she forced herself to meet his leaden eyes she saw the whiteness about his nose and mouth—less easily controlled than the velvet texture of his voice—and knew that he wasn't just angry, he was absolutely furious with her.

His jacket had been discarded, his tie pulled loose about his neck. Now he leaned back against the door, filling the space as if to bar any further attempt at escape. He was definitely not impressed with her cool query.

'Please don't play the innocent, Elizabeth. Those big blue eyes may fool the rest of the world, but they don't fool me for one minute. You assumed that without the safety net of a pre-marital contract I'd back off, let you off the leash to pursue another woman's husband.'

Lizzie, sitting in the relaxed, careless pose that she had so carefully arranged as a defence against his anticipated wrath, was shaken from her outward composure. Not by his accusation of duplicity—that was to be expected. It was far worse than that. Because he had been so determined to get his own way and marry her, she had never even considered the possibility that he might back out. When pride had carried her through the door of the solicitor's office she hadn't been thinking of anything beyond her determination not to sign his wretched contract.

'It was...' It was not like that—that was what she had been going to say. But she caught herself just in time. Having constantly protested that she did not want to marry him, what else was he to think? Now, if she backed down too quickly, buckled under and signed his nasty piece of paper, his suspicions would be aroused. But she had to say something. He was regarding her frostily down the length of his long, thin nose, waiting for her to speak.

'It was... *what*, Elizabeth? Tell me. I really can't wait to hear.'

She lifted her shoulder in an offhand little shrug. 'It was... worth a chance.'

'And?'

She looked at him as if she had no idea what he was talking about. She wished she hadn't. 'I don't understand.'

'I think you do.' He pushed himself away from the door, took a step towards her. 'Since you must have anticipated that, having gone to such lengths to keep you, I was hardly likely to let you go quite that easily...'

It was as if she had been cast in a role from which there was no escape, a part where no depth was too low for her to sink into. Well, if that was what it took, she would do her very best to oblige him. 'And,' she agreed a little defiantly, bright red spots staining her cheeks, 'it wasn't enough.'

There was a certain grim satisfaction about his mouth, and she knew that she had told him exactly what he'd expected to hear. 'A hundred thousand pounds for each year of your time with me, and all the clothes you can wear? You were anxious to get a job, Elizabeth, and I congratulate you on your good fortune. I can't imagine that even in your wildest dreams you could have conjured up anything that paid as well. But evidently it's not enough.'

He joined her on the sofa, crossed one leg over the other, propping ankle on knee, and regarded her dispassionately. 'So, my sweet, innocent little Lizzie, shall we haggle for a while, or do you have a sum in mind?'

She shifted away from him, as far as the arm of the sofa would let her go, and wrapped her arms protectively about her legs. Why did it all have to be so horrible? She swallowed unhappily. 'Perhaps we should leave it for the courts to decide what's appropriate...'

'That's a cop-out, my dear. State your price. I'd be interested to know just how much you think you're worth.'

'I would have thought it was more a question of what *you* are worth,' Lizzie retaliated.

He smiled then. But it wasn't a very nice smile. 'Yes, I suspected that was the way your mind was working.' He shrugged. 'I'm going to have to disappoint you. Sign the agreement as it stands, Elizabeth, or throw yourself upon the mercy of the courts if you think you can do better. It's your risk.'

It didn't matter one way or the other. She wouldn't touch a penny of his money, but she would never put her name to that agreement. 'Then let's leave it to the courts, shall we? I'm sure they'll be fair.'

'I'm sure they will, and the more I pay my lawyers, the fairer they'll be.' And he smiled. He was pleased with himself. 'You realise, of course, that you'll have to be very, very good if you want to see a penny of my money?'

'Good?'

'Well-behaved. Not just discreet, Elizabeth. Celibate. For every day of two and a half years while you gather your injured innocence about you. I can have all the fun I want, but for you there won't even be the consolation prize of an affair with your favourite banker.' His satisfaction was palpable. 'I'm almost tempted to take the vow of celibacy myself and force you to wait the full five years. It's going to be a tough choice, Elizabeth. What do you want most? Peter Hallam or my money?'

She didn't want either. Whatever rose-coloured spectacles she had viewed Peter through had been wiped clear by his appalling behaviour. As for Noah's money...she didn't want that either. But it was clearly pointless to say so. In fact, it wouldn't suit her purpose at all. She lifted the glossy, sun-streaked hair from the back of her neck and let her head fall back against the sofa cushion.

'A celibate wife,' she murmured. 'Well, it probably beats typing for a living. You should have offered it to me as a job, Noah. I'm sure a contract of employment would have been a great deal cheaper than—'

She broke off as his eyes narrowed dangerously. 'It wasn't my intention to be cheap.'

'No, indeed. But your intentions are beginning to baffle me. Why would Francesca Hallam's happiness be worth a quarter of a million pounds to you? You're rather cynical for such a quixotic gesture. Or does that smooth exterior hide a marshmallow heart after all? Maybe you'd have done the same for me if the situation had been reversed—married Francesca to protect my—?'

'No!' Angry colour suffused his cheek-bones.

Stunned by the fierceness of his response to her teasing question, Lizzie stared at him. What was it about Francesca that provoked such a protective reaction in him? Could it be that this man who protested that he never involved himself with married women, didn't believe in love, had fallen for the dark, fragile beauty of Peter's wife? And was this his way of demonstrating it? The idea should have seemed ridiculous. But it didn't. It was oddly painful.

Noah, as if sensing that he had overreacted, gave a little shrug. 'You have no need of my protection, Elizabeth. Or have you forgotten you have a track record for trying to upset marital harmony?' Lizzie started guiltily. She hadn't given her father one thought in the past two days and Noah, seeing her reaction and misunderstanding it, said, 'I rest my case.'

'Have you spoken to Olivia?'

'She telephoned this morning to offer her congratulations.' There was something in the tone of his voice that suggested something rather different.

Lizzie lifted her head. 'Congratulations or commiserations?'

'Commiserations?' He shrugged. 'Hardly that. She's been trying to marry me off for years. She expressed one or two reservations, perhaps.'

'To put it mildly.'

'After what she's had to put up with from you I think she was remarkably restrained. She wondered, for instance, if you were a little too young, which rather amused me.'

She blushed at this reference to her own less than convincing objection to her father's marriage. 'And?'

His eyes were quite expressionless. 'And that you were, perhaps, rather innocent for a big, bad wolf like me.'

Lizzie swallowed. 'That was all?'

'Yes. She's a generous woman. I told her that time would sort out the first problem and that I would assuredly deal with the second.' He regarded her dispassionately. 'She made me promise to be . . . kind.'

'And will you be?'

His eyes glittered angrily. 'Behave yourself and I'll be Prince Charming.'

'I think you've strayed into the wrong fairy tale,' she snapped.

'Is that right? And which particular role did you have in mind for me?'

'The Beast?' she offered.

'And you are Beauty?' He regarded her with eyes devoid of expression. 'I think I should warn you that it will take more than a kiss to tame me.'

'Then we'd better do some work on the job description to make sure we both know exactly where we stand.' His mouth tightened, but she was beyond caring. 'Let's see. Wife for short-term contract. Comfortable living quarters. Some entertaining. No housework...' she gave him a pointed look '...or children. Own room and use of car. Generous salary. That's all pretty straightforward.'

She paused, breathing rather heavily. 'Now for the difficult stuff. What did you have precisely in mind for the night-shift?'

His hand flashed out and covered her mouth, and his weight bore her back against the cushions of the sofa.

'I've never paid for a woman before,' he grated, his eyes angry slits. His thumb pressed hard across her lips, bringing the blood to the surface, making them throb. 'I wonder what you get for that kind of money?' Lizzie, already near the end of her tether, boiled over and sank her teeth into his hand.

He swore, jerking his hand away. 'You damned little vixen! You've drawn blood!'

'Perhaps you'd like me to kiss it better?' she demanded furiously, struggling to free herself. But even as she said it she recalled the impulsive way she had kissed his hand before. As his eyes darkened she knew that Noah had remembered too, and she became very still beneath him, very aware of his raised breathing rate, the pounding of his heart pressed against her breast, that special male scent mixed with the faint citrus note of cologne that was Noah Jordan.

He thrust his hand towards her face. 'Yes,' he said thickly. 'Kiss it better.' His fingers were long, the nails beautifully kept, and she found herself imagining dizzily what it would be like to be caressed by such a hand. To have her breasts cradled in those long, sensitive fingers. To feel the firm stroke of his palm across her stomach...

She drew in a sharp, shuddering breath, shocked by the intensity of such thoughts, the unexpected desire... No, that wasn't true. The desire had been there from that first kiss. He seemed to have jolted something loose in her brain then, because she hadn't been behaving quite like herself ever since...

Lizzie ducked her head so that he should not read the hunger that she was certain must be blazing from her eyes as brightly as the lights in Piccadilly Circus. Hesitantly she touched the broad pad of his thumb with her own, to wipe away the tiny drop of blood that had oozed from the puncture mark her teeth had made.

The touch was small yet hauntingly intimate. It was as if that tiny contact had sparked some connection between them—a fuse that had been there all the time, underlying the constant flare of antagonism, that had only needed a spark to set it off on an unstoppable trail of destruction. And as she touched her lips to the spot she felt the searing betrayal of a blush colour her cheekbones.

'Elizabeth?' She didn't dare look, afraid that she had misread that look in his eyes. Then he captured her throat, cupping it in the warm, curved palm of his hand, tilting her face towards him, and his thumb began gently to caress the pulse that throbbed beneath her jaw. His touch was hypnotic, its power shimmering through her body like an electric charge as his dark, heavy-lidded eyes smoked with desire.

She raised her hand to touch his face, touch the skin drawn tight across the bones of his cheeks, trail the tip of her thumb across the fierce promise of his mouth, slightly parted to reveal the tip of his tongue.

Without warning something seemed to explode inside Lizzie, burning up her lips, tightening the peaks of her breasts against the delicate lace of her bra, kindling the blissful ache of desire low in her abdomen. There was a moment of exquisite agony as he kept her waiting, suspended, it seemed, between heaven and hell, then with a shudder that racked through him his mouth descended and her lips parted on a soft groan to drink him in.

His earlier kisses had stirred her. But he had been in control then, making a point. Now, as his tongue tormented her, seeking the sweetness of her mouth, she knew it was different. Gloriously, wonderfully different. Noah was no longer in control. He couldn't help himself any more than she could.

He felt her tremble and swore softly, almost angrily as his hands caught at the hem of her blouse, tugging it over her head to fling it away. There was a moment then when she might have contained the passion—a small, still moment while his eyes drank in the soft glow of her skin, the swell of her breasts. Then, quite deliberately, she unfastened the clip between her breasts and let her bra fall away.

She had no recollection of how they disposed of the remainder of their clothes. This was no long-drawn-out seduction. There were no endless, tormenting moments while buttons were unfastened to expose the delicate curves of her body to his lips, his tongue, the gentle grazing of his teeth. There were no sweet words, no tender caresses. It was a fierce and furious mating of two people in the grip of something quite beyond them.

She screamed as he drove into her, but with triumph, not with pain. It was only afterwards that there was pain, and that had nothing to do with the rupture of a delicate membrane. It was wild and barbaric, and always, always she would know that it had been one of the most special moments in her life.

She came finally to rest on the Chinese rug in the centre of the room and lay there breathless, pinned beneath him. Then she began to laugh. It was euphoria, the sheer wonder of it. 'Is it always like that?' she wanted to know.

Noah raised himself upon one elbow and stared down at her. 'No. It's not always like that.' Then his face closed and he rolled over and sat up. 'Normally I make it to the bedroom.' He stood up and threw his shirt to her. 'Put this on; you'll get cold.'

As he turned away to pull on his trousers Lizzie suddenly felt very naked. For a moment she had thought it was going to be all right, that he had felt the glory of it too. She tugged the shirt on and wrapped it about her. Clearly it had been nothing special for him.

'You'd better go and get dressed, Elizabeth.'

The chill was back in his voice. For one crazy moment she had thought that he would carry her up to his bed and make love to her again—slowly this time, so that she could relish every moment. Crazy. Why would he do that? 'Yes.' And she shivered. 'If you'll excuse me.'

'In one of your glamorous new dresses. We're going out to dinner.'

She knew that Mrs Harper had been given the night off, but there was no need to go out. She didn't want to go out. She wanted to curl up in her own bed in her childish grey and white striped pyjamas and try to pretend that nothing had happened. 'I'll cook something,' she offered a little desperately.

'What did you have in mind? A few oysters, perhaps, before you practise your seduction techniques again?' He began to gather the rest of their clothes, giving her an unrestricted view of his athletic figure, his well-muscled back, marked by her raking fingers. Unconsciously she reached out to touch him, but he turned and saw her and she snapped her hand back as if caught trying to steal a child's sweets. 'I don't think so. Besides, it's a long-standing invitation.'

'Invitation?' He expected her to go to someone's home and eat as if nothing had happened? 'Then they won't be expecting me,' she said.

'They'll be expecting someone.' Some glamorous woman—an actress or model. Not little Lizzie French, up from the country, she thought. 'To take someone else two days before I marry you might look a little odd.' He picked up her trousers. 'I'm afraid I've ruined your new suit.'

'It doesn't matter.' She wasn't likely to wear it again. 'I haven't done your skin much good.' She touched a scratch that zigzagged across his shoulder.

'Don't!' He flinched away from her touch, his jaw clamped angrily. 'I knew that cool act hid dynamite the moment I first set eyes on you. I can certainly understand why Hallam finds it difficult to tear himself away. That was some performance. And at least the reason for the hasty wedding is now fact, rather than fantasy.'

He hadn't realised. In the white heat of their love-making it had never occurred to him that she had been a virgin. 'Peter and I—'

'It really doesn't matter,' he said, cutting across her before she could finish. Then he seemed to gather himself. 'Virgins, my dear, are a dead bore. Whatever else you may be, you certainly aren't that.'

'Does that mean you're considering an upgrade to my job description?' she demanded, clutching her clothes in front of her.

'It would certainly solve the problem of concealing our separate sleeping arrangements.' He opened the door.

'You'd better go and get in a warm bath. You're shivering.'

But not with cold. 'Would you care to join me?' she offered, glowering at him.

He smiled a little grimly. 'I'm sure you have an interesting line in bathtime games, but we're due in Eaton Square in less than an hour.'

News of their impending marriage had preceded them. Although conversation buzzed around the table, Lizzie was aware that she was the focus of curious glances, speculation. She didn't care. She felt utterly numb, responding to her neighbours' chatter but instigating none. Hardly the ideal dinner guest, she thought.

As soon as there was movement away from the table and she could extricate herself from a conversation about a new play that she hadn't seen and never wanted to, she excused herself and escaped to the dressing room set aside for the ladies. But others had had the same idea. The door was half-open, and as she put her hand on it to push it wide she heard voices.

'Hardly believe it! The mighty Noah Jordan finally hooked.'

'I can understand why. She is lovely...so fresh.'

'A bit quiet, I thought.'

'He was quiet too. They both seemed a little shell-shocked. Did you notice the way they're so careful not to meet each other's eyes? I guarantee they came straight from bed—'

'And are going right back there. I heard Noah tell Mark he had to leave early because he's flying to New York...' There was indulgent laughter.

Lizzie fled back to the drawing room before they could discover that they had been overheard, and, sure enough, very shortly afterwards Noah made their excuses and they left.

'How could you do that?' she said angrily as they drove the short distance home.

'Do what, Elizabeth?'

'Leave before anyone else. Everyone in that room will think we can't wait to get back into bed.'

'They thought that anyway. And you looked...fragile. I didn't think you could take much more.'

'Maybe you're right,' she said tightly. 'What with one thing and another it's been one hell of a day.' And she stared out of the window until he pulled into the mews.

She waited while he locked the car away and then allowed him to take her arm and escort her back across the garden and into the house. Once there, however, she left him to deal with the burglar alarm, making her way swiftly through the kitchen, determined to get to her own room and lock the door.

'Elizabeth, wait...' He caught her arm as she began to run. 'Wait,' he demanded.

'What do you want, Noah?' To her horror she realised that her voice was shaking, her legs were like jelly.

'I want to tell you that I'm—'

Lizzie winced, shrank away from him. 'Don't!' She ignored the concern that lined his face. 'Don't you dare tell me that you're sorry!' She wrenched her arm free. 'Do you hear me?'

'I hear you, Elizabeth.' He took a step back, raked his fingers through his hair. 'I just wanted you to know that I'm going to New York tomorrow. I won't see you until Thursday. That's...all.'

For a moment Lizzie remained rooted to the spot. Then she turned and fled up the elegant curve of the stair, not pausing to see whether she was pursued, locking the door to her room. Then she collapsed against it, knowing that it was all pointless. She hadn't locked the door to her heart, and it was too late now to slam the bolt home.

'Lizzie?' She opened her eyes slowly, knowing that there was some good reason not to face the day.

'Lizzie, wake up, darling.'

She turned, blinked. 'Olivia? What on earth are you doing here?'

'Noah rang some time around dawn and asked me to come up. You're going to come and stay with me at the flat until Thursday.'

She shifted, and the heavy ache of her thighs, the soreness made her wince. 'There's no need,' she said. 'Dad needs you.'

'He's coming up this afternoon. Here, I've brought you a cup of tea. Drink it while I go and get some salt for your bath.' Lizzie blushed furiously, and as she stood up Olivia touched her cheek. 'I told him to be gentle. But innocents like you are so few and far between these days...'

'He didn't know.'

'Didn't know? How could he have ever doubted?' She shook her head. 'Men are such idiots. Do you want me to tell him?'

'No,' Lizzie said quickly, lifting her shoulders in an unconsciously helpless gesture. 'He said virgins were a dead bore.'

'Did he now?' Olivia laughed. 'And did he think you were boring?' she teased.

'He said I was a lot of things, but not boring.'

'Then he shows some sense. Oh, darling, you cannot imagine how happy I am. I just knew you were made for each other.'

'You knew—?'

'Oh, yes. I knew you were the perfect wife for Noah the moment I set eyes on you. Although I have to admit I thought it would take him a little longer to realise that fact for himself. Men are usually so slow, don't you find?'

'Some men,' Lizzie replied, with a flicker of anger as she remembered what this woman was doing to her father.

'You're cross with me.' She stood up and paced towards the window, turning back with that beautifully judged movement, the restrained use of gesture that was her trademark. 'You've every right to be. I know I shouldn't have done it, but since there's no harm done... Oh, Lizzie, it's just so perfect.' And to Lizzie's astonishment she saw a tear brighten the other woman's eye. It was a quite stunning performance.

She scrambled out of bed, ignoring her aches as she pulled her dressing gown over her pyjamas. 'Olivia, what have you done?' she demanded.

'Told a rather large white lie.' She looked so repentant that if she hadn't known her stepmother better Lizzie would have laughed. 'I had to. Noah is too well acquainted with my penchant for matchmaking.' Lizzie took a step back. 'Oh, Lizzie! Don't look so disapproving. It's time he was married or he'll end up like our father—marrying someone far too young, far too late—'

'Tell me what you've done, Olivia,' Lizzie demanded. She knew, but she wanted the other woman to say it out loud. To admit it.

'Does it matter now?'

'Unless you tell me, I shan't know,' she insisted.

Olivia shrugged. Not an ordinary shrug like anyone else, but a delicate, diffident little movement of her shoulders. 'I told him that you were being ... difficult.'

' "Difficult"?'

'Well, I may have put it a *bit* stronger than that, but when I first suggested that he might have you stay for a week or two after we came back from honeymoon he was so-o-o suspicious—'

'Difficult about what, Olivia?'

'About my marriage to your father. I felt so guilty about that, because you were truly wonderful, made me so welcome.'

'I just want Dad to be happy. That's all I've ever wanted. He's had a bad time—' She stopped a little awkwardly, not knowing how much Olivia knew.

'I know all about his depression after your mother was killed in that accident—all that guilt because she was dead and he was alive...'

'I wasn't sure if he had told you. He's very sensitive about it. People can be so cruel...'

'There's no place for secrets when you love someone. James knows how much he owes to you, Lizzie—how much you've given up for him.'

No, he didn't. He didn't know about the times Peter had begged her to go away with him, the times he had asked her to marry him. 'I...couldn't bear him to be hurt again, Olivia.'

'Well, he's got two of us to bolster him out of his black moods now.' She touched her waist with a little smile. 'Three soon. And Noah.'

Noah. 'You were telling me what you said to Noah,' Lizzie said quickly, swallowing hard.

'Do I have to?'

Lizzie didn't answer.

'Yes, I suppose I do. Right. Well, I told him that you resented having to surrender Dove Court to me, kept interfering whenever I spoke to one of the staff—that sort of thing. The wretch wasn't in the least impressed with that. Not a jot of sympathy did I get. He said he was sure that I would think of some way to handle it so as not to hurt your feelings. *Your* feelings, you notice. So...' She took a deep breath.

'Well, I sighed a little. You know—one of those if-only-you-knew-the-half-of-it sighs.' A gentle ripple of laughter escaped her lips. 'I deserve an Academy award for my performance—truly, Lizzie. Lord, but I was reluctance itself. *So* understanding about the way you must be feeling. I made him coax it from me word by word—the way you spied on me, listened to my phone calls, tried to blacken my character with your father, anything to stop me marrying him.'

Lizzie paled.

'Oh, my dear, don't look so tragic. If I had told him I'd found him the perfect wife he would have run a mile. Noah is—was—the world's most dedicated bachelor.'

The woman was either totally innocent or the most consummate actress ever. And she had a sideboard groaning with awards for her performances on the stage.

'The final touch was when I expressed grave doubts about his marrying you. Men can always be relied upon to do the opposite of what they're told. Now, don't you think I was clever?'

'Very clever, Olivia. I think you're probably the cleverest woman I've ever met,' Lizzie said.

CHAPTER EIGHT

LIZZIE didn't see Noah again before the wedding. Olivia bore her away to her apartment, fussed over her, took her shopping to all her favourite boutiques and, clutching James French's credit cards, swept aside Lizzie's desperate protestation that she really didn't need a dream outfit for a quiet wedding with just a few witnesses present.

'The wedding dress isn't for the guests, my sweet, it's for Noah. It should be special. He deserves it.'

And what on earth could Lizzie say to that? So she submitted to the gentle bullying, and even she had to admit that the pencil-slim skirt and tiny jacket of the suit that Olivia finally declared exquisite was just that, the old ivory of the silk perfect against her peachy complexion. The matching hat—a delicate confection of silk leaves—completed the outfit to Olivia's total satisfaction.

They moved on relentlessly—underwear, a more expensive wardrobe of day clothes than Lizzie had ever thought possible, and evening clothes to dream about. And everywhere they were treated like stars. It should have been heaven. Her stepmother was clearly having the time of her life, and Lizzie made a valiant effort to match her enthusiasm. But Olivia could hardly fail to notice how pale she was.

'Come along,' she said finally, cutting short a visit to her favourite shoe shop. 'I'm taking you home to put your feet up, or you'll look washed out tomorrow.'

'It's you who should be putting your feet up,' Lizzie protested guiltily. Olivia had been so kind, so obviously thrilled about the wedding, that it had seemed impossible that she could be the same terrible creature Lizzie had overheard on the telephone. Maybe her father had been right after all. Maybe it had all been a dreadful misunderstanding. She really wished it could be so.

Olivia smoothed her hand over her waistline. 'The baby is fine, I promise.'

Mention of the baby sent Lizzie's thoughts winging to Francesca, wondering if she had yet told Peter the good news. Then her forehead creased in a perplexed frown. How had Noah known that she was pregnant? He had referred to Peter's impending fatherhood with such certainty...

It was a relief to be back at the flat, and while Harper carried up the endless parcels Olivia insisted that Lizzie put her feet up on the sofa while she went to organise some tea. Noah had probably just put two and two together, she thought, closing her eyes. He was good at that.

'Look, Lizzie, Noah sent flowers for you. They came while we were out.' She opened her eyes slowly and Olivia handed her a spray of red roses. For a moment her heart leapt as she slipped the card out of its envelope. 'Thursday, Noah.' That was all—a reminder, or a warning, wrapped up in the kind of gesture that his sister would expect. After all, you wouldn't expect Prince Charming to overlook anything as basic as flowers during even the briefest parting from his love.

She pushed the card back into the envelope with a little gasp.

'Lizzie? Whatever is the matter?'

'Nothing,' Lizzie said desperately. 'It's nothing. Nerves, perhaps.' How could she begin to explain that to have married Noah when she didn't love him would have been bearable. Just. A simple contract that meant nothing. Marrying him after that all too brief moment of ecstasy in his arms was more than flesh and blood could stand.

'Oh, Lord, come here, child.' And Olivia put her arms about her and let her weep.

Time, always a fickle friend, that lagged before the most eagerly awaited treats, flew swiftly to Thursday morning.

It was only when the hairdresser had left and Olivia had applied an extra touch of blusher to her pale cheeks that Lizzie had a moment for quiet contemplation of the step she was taking.

She stared at the mirror. She saw a perfectly ordinary girl who had thought she was in love with a perfectly ordinary man. A man she had known for years, ever since he'd rescued her from the village pond, and whom she had subjected to the kind of hero-worship that few boys were capable of resisting.

She had never considered that what she had felt for Peter might have been anything other than love. And in a way it had been love—the love of an impressionable little girl. Never, not even in her wildest imagination, could she conceive of responding to him with the raw passion that Noah had evoked.

It was so obvious now that the spark had always been missing, the fuse, the dynamite. And because she had stayed at home to look after her father, never met anyone to compare him with, she had never discovered that what she'd felt for Peter had been simply loving friendship.

'Lizzie, I'm just leaving...' Olivia paused in the doorway, then came into the bedroom. 'Shall I fix your hat for you before I go?'

Lizzie started, came back to reality. 'Thank you. I seem to be all fingers and thumbs.'

'Well, I dare say Noah will give you hand with the hooks and eyes later, if you ask him nicely,' Olivia replied, with a teasing smile as she set the creation of silk leaves on Lizzie's upswept hair. 'Oh, my dear,' she murmured, 'you are so beautiful I could weep. Please don't ever break my poor brother's heart.'

'Didn't you know?' Lizzie responded with a rather brittle brightness. 'Your brother professes not to have a heart.'

Olivia's face creased slightly in concern. 'He hides it well beneath that cynical exterior. But surely you of all people must know that it's just a shell. Protective armour?' Lizzie was unable to speak.

Misunderstanding her silence, Olivia sat down beside her. 'He hasn't told you?' Then she went on, 'No, he wouldn't. He was only seven when our mother fell in love with someone else, Lizzie.'

Lizzie stared at her. 'She had an affair?'

'Not just an affair. She left us. Went away one day and never came back.' She paused. 'It was a grand passion. I was into *Anna Karenina* and *Madame Bovary* at the time, and I'm ashamed to confess that the drama of it all thrilled me witless. I willingly cast my poor father as the boring older husband...' She sighed. 'I hope she was happy. They didn't have long. They died together in a hurricane.'

'A hurricane?'

'He was an American. They lived in Florida.'

'Noah took it badly?'

'Dad got him to write and beg her to come back. Unforgivable, of course, because when she didn't Noah felt so utterly rejected ... It's not that he's incapable of love, as one poor girl he discarded once suggested. He's just never found anyone he could trust with his heart. Until now.' She glanced at her watch. 'Time to go.' She touched Lizzie's cheek. 'Be happy.'

The arrival of Elizabeth Mary French at the register office for her marriage to one of London's favourite bachelors was greeted by a barrage of flashbulbs.

As she started nervously on her father's arm he squeezed her hand reassuringly and paused to let the photographers get their pictures. He seemed to have recovered all his old self-assurance, she thought; he had lost that gaunt, haunted look. At least, for now, he was happy, and right now it took all her self-possession to handle her own personal nightmare.

'Ready, sweetheart?' he asked.

She took a tighter grip on the silver Victorian flower-holder, with its spray of creamy freesias and tiny crimson rosebuds that Noah had sent her that morning. 'Yes, I'm ready.'

There were more people than she had expected gathered in the little room—faces from home—but she only had eyes for Noah. In a superbly cut dark suit, white shirt and a sober dark red tie he stood out head and shoulders, it seemed, from the crowd as his dark head turned at her arrival. He was very still, very grave. Then he extended his hand to her, and in that moment of silence before she took that last, irrevocable step she heard Peter's sharply indrawn breath.

A reminder of why she was there, it drove her forward to surrender her hand to this man who so despised her. For a moment it lay there, small and cold, then, with the most courtly gesture, he raised it to his lips.

'Miss French? Mr Jordan?' The registrar's brisk voice broke the almost palpable tension. 'Will you come this way?'

The wedding service was short, almost brutally to the point. Afterwards they ran the gauntlet of the Press once more, who were this time eagerly demanding a kiss from the newly-weds for their greedy cameras.

Noah glanced down at her. 'Do you mind?'

'Do you?' He seemed slightly taken aback by her response. In answer to her question he took her face in his hands and kissed her quite breathless. Then Olivia and James appeared behind them on the steps and Olivia played to her adoring gallery, giving Noah and Lizzie an opportunity to escape to the waiting limousine.

'A few moments of peace. We'd better cherish them; there won't be many more today,' Noah said, then turned to her. 'You look quite lovely.'

'But only down as far as my skin.'

'Elizabeth...' He picked up her hand where it lay on the seat between them, but she snatched it away. She wouldn't be patronised. Or used because he thought he had her, bought and paid for. He had made his feelings clear enough. And as for hers—well, she would have to live with them. But there would be no more close encounters of the kind that left her bereft of her self-esteem.

'What happens now?' she asked.

He hesitated, clearly wanting to say more. Then he shrugged. 'Mrs Harper will have made us a light lunch. Then she'll retire discreetly while we—'

'I thought you would be needed at the gallery this afternoon,' she said quickly.

'I'm sorry to disappoint you, but my staff have worked themselves into the ground to make sure I have this afternoon with my bride.' He touched her cheek with his fingers, turned her to face him. 'We could always spend the time in a game of chess?' he offered.

'A warlike game of move and countermove? How very appropriate. But it's hardly a long-term solution to the problem.'

'Maybe we should go down to the cottage. At least we'll be on our own there.'

'Great.'

'You don't find the proposition appealing? Well, perhaps you could stay on after the weekend. At least until Wednesday. I'll think of some good reason why—'

'What's happening on Wednesday?' she interrupted.

'You wanted to go to an auction, remember?'

'Oh. Yes.' Her eyes flickered to his. 'And will I be allowed to return to the cottage afterwards?'

'We'll see.' He turned away. 'We've arrived. Try and look as if you're happy.'

'An unhappy bride would doubtless be a terrible blow to your reputation.'

'I could live with that. But if you throw a fit of the sulks Mrs Harper will almost certainly think it's something she has done.'

And, since Mrs Harper was waiting at the door to offer her congratulations and best wishes, Lizzie did her best to comply. Then she put down her flowers and walked across to the dining room. 'How are things progressing for this evening?' she asked. 'I really should have been here...' She ran out of words as she took in the extraordinary sight of the dining room decked in flowers, the table stretched to its full length and laid with heavy silver, the finest china and the sparkle of crystal.

'No. We're all under control, despite the extra numbers. There's a pile of presents for you. Mr Jordan said to put them in the drawing room.' Lizzie followed the woman.

'Good grief! Who are they all from?'

'I've made a list. When you've finished looking at them I've laid a table for you in the morning room. I hope you don't mind, Mr Jordan, only the dining room...'

'That's fine, Mrs Harper,' he said absently. 'Why don't you serve it now? We'll be there in a moment.'

'Oh, Noah! This is awful,' Lizzie said, as soon as Mrs Harper withdrew. 'I hadn't considered...'

'Hadn't you?' He turned over a label. 'This one is from Francesca and Peter.' He picked it up and shook it. 'I wonder what it is?'

'Stop it!'

He shrugged and put it down. 'Keep a note of who they're all from if you insist. Then you can send them back. Afterwards,' he added a little grimly. 'Let's have some lunch.'

'I'm not hungry,' she murmured as the awful reality of what they had done began to sink in.

'But I am.' He offered his hand. 'Best smile, Mrs Jordan.'

'For Mrs Harper?'

'If that helps.'

She tried. And she really tried to eat, but her mouth wasn't co-operating and her throat was refusing to swallow.

'Can I get you anything else? A little fruit, perhaps?' Mrs Harper suggested, clearly concerned as she took away Lizzie's barely touched lunch.

'It's all right, Mrs Harper, I think we've just about finished here,' Noah intervened, standing up. 'Elizabeth.'

Lizzie rose slowly to her feet. 'Thank you, Mrs Harper. It was all lovely; I just couldn't—'

'Don't you fret, Mrs Jordan. It's all the excitement, I expect. You just go and have a lie down.'

'Yes, I will.' Then, blushing furiously as she realised just what that meant, Lizzie dropped her napkin onto the table and hurried across the room, not waiting for Noah to open the door, running up the stairs towards her room.

'Where are you going?' Noah's voice brought her abruptly to a halt. He was standing by the entrance to his own room, and as she turned to face him, he opened it. 'This way, Mrs Jordan.'

Her skin turned to goose flesh. He couldn't expect... It wasn't part of the deal... 'I...I'd rather use the guest room.'

'You're no longer a guest,' he reminded her, and opened the door. Very slowly, as if wading through treacle, she began to walk back towards him. It seemed to take for ever, but all too soon the door closed sharply behind her, making her jump.

'You're going to have to try to play the eager bride just a little harder, Elizabeth.'

She swung round to face him. He was leaning back against the door, far too close for comfort, and suddenly Lizzie felt as if a lump of wood was stuck in her throat.

'How... how much harder?'

He raised his hand and reached out to touch her cheek with the tips of his fingers. 'Is it so very difficult?' Lizzie didn't answer. Didn't trust herself to. Noah's mouth twisted in a smile of pure self-mockery. 'Perhaps Mrs Harper was right. You should try and rest. No one will disturb you.'

His hand dropped to the doorhandle, but his eyes never left her face. 'I'll be back around six.' He made a stirring motion. 'If you could just rumple the sheets a little...' And with that he was gone, shutting the door very quietly behind him.

For a moment she remained quite motionless, wondering what would have happened if she had told him just how easy it would have been to surrender. There would have been just more of his cutting remarks in all probability. And for a moment tears of self-pity stung at her lids. Then, furious at such weakness, she stripped away her wedding finery.

'Lie down. Rest,' she muttered as she searched through her bags, stowed in the dressing room to be sorted and unpacked at leisure. Did he honestly believe that she would be able to sleep? Defiantly she flung on a pair of jeans and, tucking in her shirt, she let herself out of the bedroom. In the doorway she paused and looked back. Then she pulled a face. If he wanted his sheets rumpled, he could damn well rumple them himself.

She walked. She had no idea where, or how far. She just needed the physical sense of being in control of her own body, her own life, with nobody directing her. Ever since Noah had swept her out of the garden of Dove Court she had been dancing to his tune, faster and faster, until she could barely think. She was almost running when the blare of a car horn brought her abruptly to the realisation that she had crossed a busy road without looking left or right.

Shaking, she went into a small café and ordered a coffee she didn't want. She just needed somewhere quiet, somewhere neutral to try to decide what she should do. Just keep walking? Disappear until the hullabaloo and fuss had died down?

Lizzie thought about it for one blissful second. Walking away from Noah, from Peter, from Olivia, from the whole wretched mess of her life. It was so tempting. But she knew that in the long run it would solve nothing. She had made her bed and no matter how lumpy it was she was going to have to lie on it. Besides, she had never run away from anything. She was Mrs Noah Jordan and for the next six months she would live that lie. But on her own terms.

She finally took a taxi home and entered the hall to find Noah, his hand gripping the telephone receiver so tightly that his knuckles were white. For just a moment relief flared in his eyes and he took half a step towards her.

'Hello,' she said brightly, turning away from him to close the door behind her. 'You're back early. Unless my watch is wrong.' She glanced at it, lifted it to her ear and shook it.

He bit down hard, a muscle working powerfully at the corner of his mouth. 'Where the hell have you been, Elizabeth?'

'I'm not quite sure. Does it matter? I just felt like a walk.'

'A walk?' he demanded in total disbelief.

'Yes, a walk. One leg before the other—that kind of thing. People did it before cars became an epidemic.' She opened a dark green and gold bag, produced a flower-spattered silk tie from its interior and pressed it into his hand. 'Somehow I ended up near Harrods, so I bought you a present. Your taste in ties is so boringly conservative. Do you want the bathroom first, or can I have it?'

He brushed aside her casual dismissal of her disappearance. 'For heaven's sake, Elizabeth, you were upset... I didn't know where you were...'

'And where were *you*, Noah?' When I needed you, she thought. When I desperately needed someone to hold me and tell me that this nightmare would eventually come to an end.

He almost flinched. Then he raked his fingers distractedly through his short dark hair, shrugging awkwardly. 'I had to collect something.'

'It must have been urgent. Oh, Mrs Harper, would you send up a tray of tea, please?' She reached back, extending her hand to her husband. 'Come on, darling. It's time we were getting ready.'

For a moment he hesitated, and then he picked her up and carried her up the stairs. Inside the bedroom he held her for a moment, frowning slightly. Lizzie, a little breathless at this unexpected turn of events—a little breathless to be held so close that she could hear his heart beat, faster than normal, she thought—finally gave a little wriggle. 'You can put me down now.'

Noah dropped her to her feet. 'What was all that about?' he demanded.

'Just following instructions, darling. Trying a little harder,' she said, moving out of his reach.

'Trying...? I believe you could try the patience of a saint,' he exploded.

'I've never tried it with a *saint*,' she replied, disappearing into the dressing room.

Noah's bathroom was panelled in rich dark wood, with an enormous bath that was fitted with old-fashioned brass taps. Lizzie lay back in it with her eyes closed. The first hurdle had been overcome. She had asserted herself, but it had been touch-and-go. And there were six months of this to get through. She didn't underestimate the size of the task. A light tap at the bathroom door startled her.

'Your tea is getting cold, Elizabeth. Do you want me to bring it in to you?' Noah asked.

Lizzie immediately tensed. Then she quite deliberately forced herself to relax. The second hurdle—enforced intimacy. Well, the sooner, the better. 'Yes, please,' she said lightly, submerging herself beneath the foam. But she kept her eyes closed as the door opened and she heard the gentle rattle of china as he placed the cup on the corner of the bath. 'Thank you.'

He didn't go away, and finally she lifted her lids to find him staring down at her, a perplexed expression creasing his brow. 'If you want to use the shower, Noah, go ahead. You won't disturb me.' Not much, he wouldn't.

'No?' The corner of his mouth lifted in the suggestion of a smile. 'In that case, why don't we share the bath? It's big enough for two.'

'I'm sure you've put it to the test on numerous occasions. But never, I'm almost positive, with a barge-pole between the occupants. However, you're most welcome to try.'

His mouth twisted in a self-deprecating smile. 'Oh, well, the shower it is. Cold, do you think?'

'You've got the idea.'

He shrugged off his bathrobe and she had a brief, tantalising glimpse of his glorious body as he turned away, but her hands hardly shook at all as she reached for her tea. She was proud of herself.

And he had apparently taken the hint, leaving her to the privacy of the dressing room to get ready for the evening, taking himself off to the bedroom to dress. When, finally, she was satisfied with her appearance, she opened the door and waited until he sensed her presence.

Her dress—a midnight-blue chiffon halter-neck—hugged her body like a lover, caressing her curves, kissing her ankles as she walked. On her feet were tiny matching suede pumps. A heavy brocade tailored jacket in shades of lilac and turquoise and the vivid blue of the sapphire at her finger trailed from her hand.

'Elizabeth...' He reached for her hand, but she stepped past him. His eyes had told her everything that she wanted to know. He desired her. And she was glad, because she hoped that the next six months would be as much agony for him as they would be for her, that he would learn to regret insults about bargepoles, eventually even, perhaps, learn the folly of his belief that she would have pursued Peter despite his marriage.

As for what Olivia had done, that was not his fault. And she could almost believe that the woman was totally sincere. She had been so kind, so thrilled that her plan had apparently worked. If she hadn't overheard that conversation...

It was strange. After days of feeling everything slipping from her control she suddenly felt incredibly wise and strong. And, since she was about to make Noah very angry indeed, that was probably just as well.

'Noah, I wanted to ask you—'

'Can it wait? I have something for you.'

'Oh?'

He held out his hand. The fairy-tale pendant dripped pearls and diamonds from his fingers. 'This is yours now. It once belonged to my grandmother.' Lizzie felt a tiny, hungering pain flicker through her. It could all have been so very different—should have been.

'The queen's necklace?' She longed to feel him fasten it about her neck. But not like this. 'Good heavens, was your *grandmother* the silent-movie star with the princely lover?' she asked lightly, so that he would not see how close she was to tears.

'Turn around, Elizabeth; I'll fasten it for you,' he said brusquely.

She placed both her hands around his fingers and closed them over the necklace. 'Save your family heirlooms for a wife you can love, Noah.' She met his puzzled eyes head-on, and it took all her courage to carry on. 'What I wanted to ask you... I want to wear my locket tonight. I can put it on a ribbon if the chain hasn't been mended.'

He could not have looked more shocked if she had hit him, and the pendant clattered onto the dressing table as he discarded it, apparently no longer interested in what became of it. 'The chain was beyond repair. I have replaced it.' He opened a drawer and took out a small box which he held out to her.

Lizzie had to remind herself that she had done nothing to be ashamed of. Standing her ground, she made no move to take it; instead she turned round. 'Will you fasten it for me?' she asked, looking back over her shoulder.

'Damn it, Elizabeth—'

'If the contents of the locket matter to you so much, Noah, I suggest you open it.'

He opened the box and lifted the locket from the velvet bed. For a moment he held the bright golden oval in the palm of his hand. 'They don't matter in the least,' he said hoarsely.

And Lizzie took considerable comfort from the fact that the cool Noah Jordan spent rather a long time in the fastening of one very plain catch—for the simple reason that his hands were shaking.

They arrived at the gallery to a burst of applause from the staff. Lizzie was taken round and introduced to everyone and a bottle of champagne was broached to drink their health.

Lizzie sipped the champagne. Just a tiny sip. She wanted to keep a very clear head. Then, as the staff dispersed to their stations, Noah took her glass and said a little urgently, 'Elizabeth—'

'Oh, look, Dad and Olivia have come early. Heavens, doesn't she look gorgeous?' She left Noah's side and went over to them, kissing them both.

'Lizzie you look absolutely stunning,' her father said.

And Olivia beamed. 'I knew that dress was right for you. But I was sure you'd be wearing Grandma's fancy baubles tonight.' She dropped her voice a little. 'It was when I saw them on you in that photograph in the paper that I knew I'd got it right.' She turned to Noah. 'Why didn't you let Lizzie wear—?'

But he wasn't given a chance to defend himself before Lizzie's father intervened. 'She's wearing her mother's locket.' His eyes were a little brighter than usual as he turned to Olivia a little uncertainly. 'It was the first present I ever gave her. She wore it on her wedding day.'

She felt Noah stiffen at her side as Olivia bent to examine it. 'It is lovely. So heavy. May I peep inside?' And before Lizzie could stop her she had slipped the catch. 'Oh, Lizzie, you are so like your mother.' Then she laughed. 'James, is this really you? Your hair! It's down to your shoulders!' She turned to her husband. 'Darling, were you wearing *flares*?' she demanded. 'Look, Noah, it's absolutely hilarious.'

And Lizzie knew that Olivia had done it quite deliberately, to make her husband laugh, show him that she understood how much he had loved his first wife, that she didn't feel threatened.

Very slowly, very painfully Noah directed his eyes to the two small photographs that smiled across at each other—very hippy, very sixties.

'Hilarious,' he agreed. But he wasn't amused. Not in the least. And, without so much as a glance at Lizzie, he detached himself from the group to go and greet the first arrivals who had come to see the exhibition and meet the new Mrs Jordan.

'Elizabeth.' Noah squeezed through the crowds some time later. 'It's time to get back to the house. I've promised Fran and Peter a lift. Could you find them?'

Lizzie had glimpsed Noah talking to Fran, taking her around the exhibition, telling her about the artists. Beseiged by well-wishers, she was unable to join them, but even if she had been alone she didn't think she would have intruded. They seemed so private, so apart from the noisy chatter that filled the gallery, that her heart felt as if it was being squeezed very hard. She had looked for Peter, had seen him talking to her father, but Peter too had seemed intensely aware of the other couple, following them jealously with his eyes.

She found Fran and Peter now, and extricated them from a discussion about the economy. 'Noah said you were coming home with us. If you're ready...'

'Oh, yes. But this has been wonderful,' Fran said enthusiastically. 'I suddenly want to collect modern art.'

'I'll throw a few cans of paint at a wall for you, if you like,' Peter offered.

Fran flushed. 'Peter, for goodness' sake...'

'Well, you're not taken in by all this, are you?' he sneered. 'Or perhaps you are? You wouldn't be the only one.'

And with a sinking heart Lizzie realised that Peter wasn't referring to the paintings.

CHAPTER NINE

THE house was a glittering showcase when they arrived, and Fran was justifiably awestruck. 'It's just so beautiful, Lizzie. I'd love to look around. Is there time?'

Before she could suggest that Noah would be a better guide he intervened. 'I'll give you the grand tour when we've more time,' he promised. 'But perhaps you would like to freshen up.' He turned to Lizzie. 'Why don't you take Fran upstairs, darling, while I have a chat with Peter?'

Lizzie's heart turned a somersault. The hostility between the two men was well-disguised beneath the civilising veneer of politeness, but her nerves were strung out so tight that she was sensitive to the most subtle inflexion. 'Chat' had an almost ominous ring to it.

But Fran was blissfully unaware that anything was amiss. 'You'd better stay off the subject of art,' she advised mock-seriously. 'You may have already noticed, Noah, that my husband is a philistine.'

'Then perhaps I should try to...convert him to my viewpoint,' Noah replied, opening the study door.

'Don't bank on it,' Peter almost growled. 'Besides, there's something far more important we have to discuss—' His voice was cut off as Noah shut the door behind them.

'Come on, Lizzie.' Fran was bubbling with excitement. 'I'm absolutely dying to see this famous four-poster.'

'Famous?' Lizzie repeated dully. She remained rooted to the spot, staring at the study door, half expecting to hear the crash of furniture as the men came to blows.

'Noah's been telling me that it has quite a history,' Fran insisted.

Lizzie finally managed to drag her attention back to Fran. 'Noah has an interesting line in historical detail,' she said, and with a last glance back turned to lead the way upstairs. 'I hope it wasn't too shocking?'

Fran laughed. 'Oh, I didn't believe a word of it, but it was great fun. He's so amusing...' Her voice died away as Lizzie opened the door for her. 'Oh, Lizzie!'

The great Jacobean four-poster dominated the room. On either side tall lamps threw soft illumination over the heavy drapes and coverlet, and the tumbled creamy silk and lace of the most exquisite nightgown—a gown that Lizzie had never seen before. And everywhere there were roses, rich and darkly red, scenting the air. It was quite beautiful. Like something from a Hollywood movie. In fact, she had the strongest feeling that that was precisely what it was—a stage set. 'Why don't you take Fran upstairs, darling?' Of course. The final, convincing touch. But who was Noah trying to convince?

Fran took a step towards the bed, touched the heavy, embroidered hangings. 'You must feel like a queen, sleeping in a bed like this,' she murmured.

'I don't know about that,' Lizzie murmured absently as her fingers stirred the soft silk of the nightgown; she felt deeply disturbed by sharp desires that had bubbled up to almost choke her. 'I haven't actually slept in it...'

'Oh, Lizzie! You are outrageous,' Fran said, laughing. 'You're just trying to make me jealous!'

'No...' Then colour flooded to her cheeks as she realised what she had said, what Fran had thought she'd meant. 'I'd better get downstairs,' she said quickly.

'People will be arriving any minute. The bathroom is through there. Can you find your own way back down?'

Noah was standing at the foot of the stairs as Lizzie descended. 'Well, was she impressed?'

'How could she fail to be?' Confirmation that all that effort had been expended to reinforce Francesca's sense of security sent a cold, painful shiver through her. 'Where is Peter?' she asked quickly, not wanting to dwell on the unexpected intensity of her feelings. 'What have you been saying to him, Noah?'

Noah regarded her with a slightly puzzled expression. 'I think you should be worrying about what he said to me.'

Lizzie paled. 'What?'

He raised his hand to her shoulder and briefly trailed his fingers across her skin. 'I like this dress.'

The simple touch of his fingers seemed to rob her of the ability to think, to breathe. The sight of his bedroom—their bedroom—that nightgown...had shaken her new-found purpose. She glanced uncertainly up into his eyes. They glittered darkly back at her, offering no clue to his feelings. And she remembered with a jab of pain that, for him, nothing had changed. Any loving attention was like that bedroom—window-dressing. Just for show.

Well, she could put on a show of her own. She lifted her hand to touch the soft material that clung to her breast. 'I'm glad you like it, Noah.' And she lowered her lashes. 'It cost you a small fortune.' Then she moved forward as the door was opened to the first of their guests.

The evening was the longest she could ever remember. Smiling, conversing brightly with people she had never met before, she found it almost a relief, she thought guiltily, to escape for a while when Fran, briefly overcome with dizziness, left the party early.

'Would you like me to come with you?' Lizzie offered with some concern as Peter settled her in the car.

But Fran smiled a little wanly. 'You can't leave your own wedding party, Lizzie. Peter will look after me.' She tightened her hold upon his hand. 'Won't you, honey?'

Lizzie felt almost sorry for him. Ever since his conversation with Noah he had been very quiet, glancing first at Fran and then at Noah, as if trying to make sense of something. Now he could do little other than nod.

'Take good care of her, Peter. If you need anything, give me a call. I'll ring you later.'

'Thanks, Lizzie. Thank you... for everything.' His eyes said it all. Whatever crisis his marriage had been through seemed to be passing as he realised that his wife was carrying his child.

'Is she all right?' Noah asked, coming out into the hall to find Lizzie.

There was such a tender concern in his voice that Lizzie for one crazy moment felt the most appalling flare of jealousy—foul, bilious-green jealousy. She longed for that concern, that tenderness. 'Yes. They're *both* all right. How did you know that she was pregnant?'

Noah regarded her steadily with smoky eyes that told her nothing. 'Women get a special look when they're pregnant.'

'And you're an expert?'

'I've spent a lifetime learning to use my eyes...'

'And you've done that most attentively ever since you met her.' Lizzie's eyes darkened to indigo, and she had to dig her nails into the palms of her hands to stop the tears. 'I can't imagine why you didn't encourage me to run away with Peter. Then you would have had the field to yourself.' She turned and began to move rapidly away, but his hand snapped out and stopped her.

'You have my assurance, Elizabeth, that for the rest of the evening you will have my undivided attention.' It was a promise that offered no comfort.

As the last of their guests departed Lizzie went to the phone. 'What are you doing?' Noah asked.

'Ringing Peter to see how Fran is.' Her eyes challenged him. 'I'm sure you'd like to know.'

He paused, then shrugged. 'Give her my love.'

'I'll leave you to do that yourself when you see her.'

He frowned. 'Was that supposed to mean something, or were you just being unpleasant?'

'Work it out for yourself.' She turned her back on him and punched in the number of the hotel.

'Well?' Noah had discarded his jacket, pulled his black tie loose and undone the top button of his shirt, exposing his powerful throat as he threw his head back in a characteristic gesture. He was tired. She longed to go to him, put her arms around him, comfort him . . .

She jolted herself back to reality. Just how many kinds of a fool was it possible for one person to be? 'She's sleeping. Peter said to pass on his thanks for an enjoyable evening . . . and that he'll ring in a couple of days.' She hesitated. 'What about, Noah?'

Noah, pouring brandy into a glass, waved the decanter in her direction and, ignoring her question, said, 'Can I offer you a drink?'

'No, thanks. I've had more than enough.'

'You've drunk nothing but mineral water all evening.'

She had been aware of his eyes apparently riveted upon her, but then that was all part of the game. People would expect it. It might have been his sister who was the actress, but Noah could easily have succeeded in the same profession. Only she had seen the gentler glances that Francesca had drawn from him. 'It seemed wise to keep a clear head. I would be grateful if you could manage to do the same.'

'Frankly, my dear, tonight a clear head offers very little to commend it.'

'I can sympathise with your feelings. But this little farce was your bright idea, and I would like to be reassured that, since we have to share that monstrous bed, you'll remember that it's your wife you're sleeping alongside. I wouldn't want to be confused with some more enthusiastic acquaintance.'

He turned to her. 'You're wrong, you know. I never sleep with mere acquaintances. To be honest, right now I don't even feel much like sleeping with you. And we both know how enthusiastic you are.'

It was frightening how much that hurt. 'Alongside,' she repeated, hanging onto her poise despite the hot patches that flared on her cheeks. 'Not *with*. But please don't force yourself, Noah. You're quite welcome to sleep on the sofa.'

'Sorry, sweetheart, the show must go on.' He drained the brandy in his glass and poured another, then turned to her. 'So, tell me, did you enjoy your wedding day? Did it live down to your expectations?'

'It had its moments. Mostly it was just exhausting.'

'Surely not? Not for the perfect Miss Lizzie French?' He regarded her steadily. 'You are perfect, aren't you? People keep telling me you are—your father, Peter, Francesca. Sugar and spice and all things nice. Even Olivia chose tonight to confess that she hadn't been exactly honest when she blackened your character...'

'Oh?'

'I was sharp with her for being so insensitive to James's feelings this evening. It's so unlike her.' He leaned against the sideboard. 'She thought I was cross with her for matchmaking. Since I clearly hadn't a clue what she was talking about, she had to explain. She seemed surprised that you hadn't told me.'

'There really didn't seem any point.'

'No point?'

'Would you have believed me?' She made a gesture of pure defiance. 'Have you ever believed me?'

'I don't recall you trying very hard to convince me of your probity. Not even about the locket.' He reached out and lifted it from her throat, his knuckles grazing her skin as he flipped it open. 'You made no attempt to correct my mistake. Did you?'

'In my shoes, Noah, would you have bothered to protest your innocence?'

'Maybe not,' he conceded. 'But to ask me to fasten it about your neck tonight, knowing what I thought... A nice touch.' He snapped it shut and let it fall against her skin. 'Very... human.' He took another sip from his glass.

'I've never pretended to be anything else.'

'No. And I have good reason to know just how human you can be. Don't I?'

Her skin burned at this reminder of how human her response to his lovemaking had been. No. No. Not lovemaking. Just sex. She turned abruptly away, desperate to shut out the memory of it. 'Olivia's little story was a great deal closer to the truth than she imagined,' she said quickly. Anything to distract him. 'I didn't deliberately snoop, but I did overhear a telephone conversation. She was talking to her lover—'

'Lover?'

'Telling him that she was keeping on her apartment in London so that she could meet him there—a married man, apparently, since she was particularly pleased to have convinced my father that the child she is carrying is his.'

If she had hoped to make Noah angry, she was disappointed. He seemed, on the contrary, to be totally nonplussed. 'Olivia?' Lizzie didn't bother to answer. 'I think you'd better tell me exactly what you heard. Word for word.'

It wasn't difficult. It was burned into her brain. When she had finished he simply shook his head.

'Tell me, Elizabeth,' he said, 'if you really believe this nonsense, didn't you feel just a shade awkward spending the last three days with Olivia, letting her do everything for you...?'

'I wasn't given much choice about that.' But a deep flush darkened her cheeks.

'You must know it is some kind of misunderstanding. It isn't in Olivia's character to do anything so...deceitful.'

She gave him a wry look. 'Matchmaking aside?' Then with an awkward little shrug she added, 'You'll be happy to know that Dad took the same view.'

'You went to James with this infernal rubbish? My God, if he'd believed you—'

'But he didn't. And after tonight, the way she understood, helped him with all that nonsense over the locket, I know somehow that he must be right, that there must be some explanation—'

'Of course there's an explanation...' He spun around, turning his back to her, and stared up at the ceiling with a sharp expulsion of breath. 'I suppose I should be grateful that you aren't quite as perfect as everyone would have me believe. No one with a shred of decency could have carried on as if nothing had happened, stood as her bridesmaid—'

'Did you think I enjoyed it? I did that for my father.'

'Oh, no, Elizabeth. You did it for you.' He turned abruptly, and stabbed at her with an accusing finger. 'To get back in Daddy's good books. It must have been quite a shock to discover that you were about to have serious competition for his attention.' His hand dropped to his side. 'It's something of a relief, to be honest, to know that I needn't feel so sickeningly guilty—'

'Guilty?' She was beginning to be utterly confused. 'Noah, please don't have any more brandy.' She moved swiftly to the door. 'I'll make some coffee.'

He caught her arm, detaining her. 'I don't want any coffee. Besides, you haven't heard the best part yet.'

'Best part?' Her heart sank. It was going to get worse and she didn't think she could bear it.

'Did you know that Peter is thinking of transferring to England? He's apparently been offered a move to London, with a promotion.'

Lizzie shook off his hand and subsided wearily onto the sofa. 'He wouldn't...'

'He was a little concerned that Fran might have to give up her job if he took it. That's very touching, don't you think?' He lowered himself beside her, his legs stretching out seemingly endlessly in front of him, the warmth of his arm brushing against her shoulder. She shifted nervously away. 'Unless, of course, he thought it would be the perfect excuse to put the width of the Atlantic between them?'

'It wouldn't make any difference to me.'

He gave a hollow imitation of laughter. 'Do you know, I actually suggested that if he stayed here it wouldn't be very kind—?' Lizzie's hands flew to her mouth. 'Yes. Quite a joke. Fortunately he interrupted before I made a complete fool of myself. He thought I was going to say that it wouldn't be very kind to Fran.'

She let out a soft breath of sheer relief that after all she had been through Noah hadn't actually let the cat out of the bag. 'What did he say?' she demanded.

'He cares for you very deeply. He wanted some assurance that I wouldn't hurt you.' He grimaced. 'He apparently doubts my fibre as husband material. It took considerable self-control to allow myself to be lectured on my good fortune...' He turned to her. 'On your innocence...' Lizzie paled. She tried to say something, but her mouth seemed glued together. 'I believe I was able to reassure him that my intentions were entirely honourable.'

'That's... all right, then.'

'I'm glad you agree. Peter Hallam is a very mixed-up young man. He needs time to sort himself out.'

Lizzie nodded wearily. 'Fran had a miscarriage just after their somewhat precipitate marriage. He blamed her...' Anger flickered briefly across Noah's face before it was shuttered against her. She shivered a little, as if someone had walked over her grave. 'Hopefully this time everything will be all right. But she hasn't told him yet... You can see why...'

'Yes, I can see. But after this evening I imagine he will have worked it out for himself.' His mouth twisted in a mockery of a smile. 'Unless he's quite stupid.'

'He's not—' Lizzie stopped. Defending Peter was no longer her concern.

'Perhaps I'm being unkind. He's certainly no more stupid than I've been. There's a certain irony in the situation, don't you think?'

She hadn't noticed him move, yet somehow he seemed threateningly closer. 'I...I don't know what you're talking about.'

'I think you do. I thought I was in control—forcing you to marry me to protect Fran.'

'Giving up your precious freedom—the most noble sacrifice. Especially for a girl who was a virtual stranger.'

'Sacrifice.' He tested the word. 'Yes. I suppose that describes the situation. But apparently it wasn't my sacrifice. It was all yours.' Lizzie edged nervously towards the end of the sofa. 'You had your escape all planned. Then he begged you to go away with him. You married me as a last resort, to convince Peter that you weren't interested in him. Very noble.'

'Noble? Me?' But her biting sarcasm was lost as her voice trembled beneath his probing eyes and she gave a shaky laugh. 'You're a much better catch, after all.'

'Then why were you all packed and ready to leave, until you received a letter from him?'

She lifted her chin a little defiantly. 'He'd seen through your little game, you know. He was certain that we weren't lovers.'

'I wonder why?' The edge of Noah's voice was sharp enough to cut paper. Her eyes widened. Surely Peter hadn't been that explicit? 'You married me to convince Peter that you were no longer interested in him. You'll be glad to know that it appears to have worked.'

She was going to deny it, but suddenly it didn't seem to matter. 'He wasn't thinking straight. He thought he had been trapped into marriage, cheated. He was over-reacting to his disappointment about Fran's miscarriage.'

She shook her head. 'I don't know if his marriage to Fran will work, but I was not going to be his excuse for running away without giving it a chance. But he wouldn't listen.' Her voice had begun to tremble slightly but she pressed on. 'So I told him I was going to marry you... After all, it was what you wanted.'

Noah came back from some vast distance inside his head and threw a sharp glance at her. 'Just like that? You didn't think twice?'

Did it matter how many times she had thought about it? How she had agonised in that little café? 'Once was more than enough. We had a common purpose at last, you and I. Six months will go quickly enough.'

'I'm glad you think so. It certainly explains one thing that has been puzzling me.'

She didn't offer him a prompt. She didn't want to hear what was coming next, but there was no escape.

'It explains, my dear wife, why you didn't make any attempt to stop me making love to you. You were afraid that your overreaction to the pre-marital contract had made me think twice.'

He raised his hand and touched her lips very lightly with the tips of his fingers. Pressed hard against the corner of the sofa, she had no retreat. 'So you decided to take out a little insurance against a change of heart. The ultimate sacrifice. I only hope you think he was worth it.'

'Ultimate sacrifice?' She knocked his hand away. 'Isn't that putting it rather strong? It was just sex.'

'No, not quite. The first time is never..."just sex". I apologise that I failed to realise... Not very bright of me, but then in view of the enthusiasm of your performance you can hardly blame me.'

Performance! She rose shakily to her feet. 'What's the matter, Noah? Wasn't I boringly virginal enough for you? Do you feel cheated? Perhaps you'd like a rerun, with me fighting for my honour every inch of the way? Would you think you'd had your money's worth then?'

There was a moment of total silence, then Lizzie took an involuntary step back, and then another as Noah, almost in slow motion, uncurled from the sofa to tower above her. But it wasn't enough. Nowhere near enough. The world wasn't large enough to escape the wrath that masked his face, and she backed rapidly until brought abruptly to a halt by the door, where finally her legs gave way and she crumpled helplessly to the floor.

Then she closed her eyes, holding her head, shaking it painfully from side to side as she moaned, 'I'm sorry, I'm sorry, I'm sorry...'

He swore, a low and painful oath, before hauling her to her feet, steadying her none too gently as she rocked. Then he swung her up into his arms, holding her for just a moment, his face positively gaunt in the lamplight. She heard a voice that might have been her own, protesting feebly.

'Be quiet. You've said more than enough.' And he carried her up the stairs and deposited her upon the great four-poster bed. She wriggled frantically back against the carved headboard, certain that he intended to take her at her word. But he kept his distance. 'You shouldn't have done it.'

She swallowed. I couldn't help myself. It wasn't planned, she wanted to say. The words wouldn't come. She remembered too vividly that moment when she could have stopped him, but didn't. 'Noah...' Then, exhausted, confused, Lizzie covered her face with her hands, unable to bear his accusing eyes a moment longer.

He sank onto the bed beside her, pulling her hands away, refusing to let her hide from him. 'You love him that much?' he demanded. 'So much that you would do anything—even marry me—rather than let him make a total mess of his life?'

He had it wrong. All wrong. But nothing she could say would ever convince him of that. 'I thought it was Fran's life that was the reason for this madness, Noah.

Perhaps it's time you told me why she's so important to you.' He didn't answer. 'Are you in love with her?'

He abruptly released her hands and turned from her, raking his fingers through his hair, staring down at the carpet. 'Lord, what a mess.'

That just about covered it, Lizzie thought. But she still had her pride. 'It doesn't matter, Noah. It doesn't make any difference. You don't have to feel ... responsible ...' She faltered as he swung round and his eyes stabbed at her.

'And if you're pregnant?'

That was a possibility she hadn't dwelt upon. There was no point. Either she was or she wasn't. Nothing could change it. 'It won't be your problem, Noah. I promise you.'

'It isn't in your power to absolve me of that responsibility, Elizabeth,' he said quietly, but there was a bottomless depth to the intensity of those words. Then more gently he added, 'I'm afraid it never occurred to me that you hadn't got that angle covered.'

'I'm sorry—'

'Don't!' She flinched at the harshness of his voice. 'I don't want to hear how sorry you are.'

'Noah—' She stopped. Nothing she could say could make it better. Maybe it was better not to try.

He stood up. 'You'd better try and get some sleep, Elizabeth. You look terrible.'

It was nothing to the way she felt, but she refused to let him see that each word was like a knife-cut. 'You say the kindest things.'

'I don't feel ... kind.'

'I would have said that you don't know the meaning of the word, but I've seen you with Fran. I've seen the way you treat her like a piece of the most delicate Chinese

porcelain, look at her as if she's some kind of princess.
I don't know what it is between you two—'

'Don't!' He placed his hand over her mouth. 'You
don't know what you're talking about.' Then he shook
his head and straightened. 'Just try and sleep. I won't
disturb you. You have my promise.'

But the words had a hollow ring. She was already disturbed. Deeply, dangerously disturbed.

Lizzie woke very early, opening confused eyes to a scene
that finally resolved itself into a canopy of embroidered
flowers and birds as she became accustomed to the dim
light. Then a movement beside her warned her that
although Noah had not joined her in the long hours when
she lay awake, unable to close her eyes and shut out her
misery, she was no longer alone.

She sat up, throwing an anxious glance down at the
bed beside her. But his back was turned to her, his
breathing the slow, even pattern that indicated deep sleep,
and she was able to breathe once more. Smothering a
yawn, she very carefully eased herself back down on the
pillow. She would be safe for another half-hour and she
was so tired.

But it was no good. She couldn't go back to sleep.
Her eyes were continually drawn to the figure sleeping
beside her, half-turned onto his stomach. Drawn to the
way his thick dark hair was cut to lie smoothly into the
nape of his neck, to the way his back was bunched into
power-packed muscle by an arm thrown at an angle
across his pillow, and to the deep indentation along his
spine that disappeared at waist-height beneath the sheet.

She wanted to reach out and touch him, feel the
warmth of silky skin beneath her hands, smooth away
the cover so that she could enjoy his body without hin-
drance. Her own body reacted instinctively to the

shocking sensuality of her thoughts, her nipples peaking, an urgent tremble invading her loins.

But even as she reached out to touch the smooth, tanned skin she snatched her hand back from the brink of madness and, flinging back the bedclothes, fled to the relative safety of the bathroom, the sobering chill of a needle-sharp shower. She was shivering when she wrapped the thick, fluffy bathrobe about her. But she was safe.

She was in the dressing room, sitting at the mirror brushing her hair, when she sensed that she was no longer alone and turned to see Noah standing in the doorway, watching her.

'Hello,' he said. She didn't answer, returning to her task, but he didn't go away. He advanced upon her, filling the mirror. 'Did you sleep well?'

'Very well, thank you.' The hand with the brush dropped to her lap. Her hand was shaking too much to continue.

He pulled a face at her reflection. 'Then heaven help you when you have a bad night.' He reached for the hairbrush. 'Good Lord, you're freezing,' he said as his hand touched hers. He put the brush down and, squatting down in front of her, took her hands in his, chafing some warmth into them. Then he briskly rubbed her arms and back through the bathrobe.

'Don't,' she begged softly. 'Please, don't.'

He stopped immediately and stood up, but the agony wasn't over. 'Come on, back into bed with you,' he said.

'No, I'm...' The words disintegrated into a little scream as he bent and picked her up, striding across the room with her to deposit her upon the bed. 'Here, put this on; it will warm you up.' He held out the silk nightdress to her. She had pointedly ignored it the night before, preferring the safety of her striped cotton pyjamas.

'This is silly, Noah. I'm just going to get dressed.' He shrugged and caught the tie of her bathrobe. 'All right!' she squeaked, and slid beneath the sheets. She wriggled out of the bathrobe then, clutching the sheet up to her chin, held out her hand for the nightdress.

But, having thrown her robe over a chair, Noah chose to hold the frothy confection just out of reach, tantalising her with it. 'I'll give it to you on one condition,' Noah said softly.

'What condition?'

'The next time you feel the need for a cold shower, Elizabeth Jordan, you invite me along. It would give me considerable pleasure to witness your suffering.'

'Damn you, Noah! Give me that—'

He placed his finger over her lips. 'Not quite the attitude of a bride on the first morning of her married life—'

'I didn't *choose* to get married.'

'Didn't you? I thought we agreed last night that this was, after all, exactly what you chose.'

Lizzie glared at him. 'But... It doesn't make any difference.'

'You think not?' He sat beside her on the bed and tossed the nightdress on the floor. 'It's not as if you find me...repellent.' His fingers traced the hollow of her shoulder, and he smiled as she shivered. 'I don't believe you could act quite that convincingly.'

She edged away from him, but he had her effectively trapped, naked beneath the sheet. Suddenly Lizzie was very afraid that he was going to demonstrate precisely how different the situation was. 'Noah, please!' she begged, a little desperately.

He smiled—a little twist of his mouth that was quite terrifying. 'Please,' he repeated softly, echoing the plea in her voice. 'I liked that. Please, what?'

'Don't... play games with me.'

He regarded her thoughtfully. 'We have six months to fill. And I like... games. Did you know that you have the most beautiful neck?'

She wanted to pull the sheet higher to cover her neck, but he was sitting on it. So she slipped further down against the pillows. His smile did not reassure her. 'I'll scream if you touch me,' she said quickly.

He rolled onto his side, propped himself on his elbow and smiled lazily down at her. She could feel the warmth of his body through his silk wrap, the linen sheet.

'That rather depends where I touch you, Elizabeth.' He laid his hand lightly on her breast, teasing a betraying nipple.

'Noah!' she groaned.

'You'll have to raise your voice a little...' his cool grey eyes had an almost hypnotic quality '...if you want to summon assistance.' She didn't. That was the trouble. 'I believe you've stopped shivering, my dear. Could it be that you're feeling warmer?'

Warmer? She practically had steam coming out of her ears. 'Just a little,' she agreed, her voice little more than a croak.

'You sound as if you might be getting a cold. Perhaps you'd better spend the rest of the day in bed. I'd be happy to—' A tap at the door saved her from his opinion on the best way to spend the rest of the day. 'Come in,' Noah called.

Mrs Harper bustled in, bearing a tray of tea. 'I've brought up the papers for you, Mr Jordan, as you asked. There are some lovely pictures... Breakfast in an hour, Mrs Jordan?'

Lizzie lay helplessly trapped beneath the sheet, burning with embarrassment. His little seduction had been nothing but a cruel tease. He'd known that they would be interrupted. Next time she might just prove more willing, and let him suffer too...

'Half an hour,' Noah intervened, managing to sound infinitely regretful. 'Tell Harper that we'll want the car at ten. He'd better check the traffic to Heathrow. Our flight is at midday.'

'Yes, sir.' The moment she closed the door behind her Noah swung from the bed in one graceful movement and walked across to the table to collect the papers.

Lizzie sat bolt upright. 'Our flight? Where are we going?'

'Cairo. Just for one night. You'll need something glamorous for this evening. And something to cover up with. It can get cold once the sun goes down. As for the rest, something casual will do.' He regarded her gravely. 'But not—'

'Jeans,' she finished for him as he dumped the papers on the bed for her. 'No need to labour the point, Noah. But I thought we were going to the cottage this weekend.'

'We can go there any time. This is a once-in-a-lifetime opportunity...and my wedding present to you. I went to pick up the tickets yesterday afternoon.' He paused in the bathroom door. 'And, even if I do say it myself, it's a considerable improvement on that horrible tie.'

'Let me tell you, Noah Jordan, I spent hours choosing that tie—'

'I don't doubt it. It can't have been easy to find something that hideous.' He didn't wait for her reply, but retreated into the bathroom and closed the door. And as soon as she heard the water running Lizzie scrambled from the bed and dived into the safety of the dressing room.

The flight on Concorde was swift and thrilling for Lizzie, and the crowded, noisy city of Cairo a collage of brilliant impressions as they swept along in their chauffeur-driven car—impressions of the Nile glinting with sunlight and the feluccas plying their trade from bank to bank, of tall, white-robed figures striding majestically along the dusty roads, of cafés crowded with old men drinking mint tea from tiny glasses. Lizzie was enchanted.

'Can we see the museum? The pyramids?' she asked breathlessly as they checked into their hotel.

'You'll be seeing the pyramids tonight,' Noah informed her.

'Tonight? Oh, glory, are they floodlit?' Then a sudden tremor of excitement rippled through her. 'Noah?'

He signed the registration form, handed over their passports to the hotel receptionist and turned to Lizzie. 'I can see from your face that you've guessed my surprise. Well, I promised you I'd take you to see *Aida*. I thought perhaps you might enjoy hearing Domingo in the original setting.'

'Might enjoy...?' Lizzie, overwhelmed by his generosity, flung her arms impetuously about his neck and kissed him, heedless of the fact that they were in the reception lobby of the most opulent hotel in the capital. 'No one has ever given me a better wedding present,' she said breathlessly.

'Well, give it time, my dear. You've only been married once. Perhaps your next husband will manage *Madame Butterfly* in Nagasaki.' And he disentangled her arms from about his neck.

CHAPTER TEN

ONLY the very public nature of their location kept Lizzie's hands glued to her sides, that and the fact that if she let fly it would betray just how very much his words had hurt her. But, as if regretting his early morning flirtatiousness, Noah had been terse to the point of irritability ever since he had joined her at breakfast.

Her own excitement had carried her through the journey, but now she had no choice but to confront the fact that while she had been continually urged to keep up the appearance of a happy newly-wed Noah obviously didn't feel the same rules applied to him. Well, here no one knew or cared whether they were happy.

'It is not my intention to make a habit of collecting husbands, Noah. On present performance, six months of you will be more than enough to last me a lifetime,' she said, her voice crackling with frost, leaving him in no doubt about how angry she was. Then she turned and followed the waiting porter to the lift, not caring whether Noah followed her or not.

Their suite had two bedrooms, she saw with relief, and immediately retired to the nearest, shutting the door firmly behind her. She didn't lock it. That would have smacked of the melodramatic, and there was clearly no need since Noah made no effort to disturb her. But then she hadn't expected him to.

Lizzie spent a long time dressing. Noah had gone out of his way to remind her that this marriage was to be purely temporary, and despite her fury she knew that whatever his purpose had been in marrying her she had been guilty of using him. The least she could do was make an effort to play the part of Mrs Noah Jordan to the hilt. This morning she had come all too close...

She had brought with her a gown in floating silk chiffon that Olivia had encouraged her to buy despite the outrageous cost. It was constructed in a jewel-bright harlequin patchwork of diamond shapes supported by tiny shoelace straps, and she had fallen in love with it on sight. She wrapped the slender, toning scarf about her throat, leaving the long ends to trail behind her, and then slipped her feet into a pair of silk pumps.

But despite the brilliance of her reflection in her mirror it gave her little pleasure. The image that shimmered back at her was not Lizzie French. That pale, strained face belonged to Mrs Noah Jordan. She picked up her bag and opened the door.

Noah was on the balcony, his arms resting on the parapet, his attention wholly fixed on the traffic on the Nile. For a moment he didn't move, and her eyes softened as they lingered on his powerful figure. Then he looked over his shoulder, and his glance, detached and wintry, flickered over her briefly. 'Another fortune, I fancy,' he murmured, straightening.

'How true,' Lizzie replied, her voice apparently struggling through treacle. 'In fact, this dress was considerably more expensive...'

He conceded a grudging smile to her fighting spirit. 'It was worth every penny, I assure you. But you'll have to try harder than that if you want to make me wince,' he said, gravely mocking her naïvety. 'That *was* your intention?'

'Watch this space,' she advised him shortly.

'I will do so with pleasure,' he reassured her. 'Now, give me your wrist.'

'Why? Are you planning to slap it?'

'How tempting. But no.' He waited. A little nervously she extended her hand to him, then stared in disbelief as he fastened a bracelet—a strand of uncut diamonds, each one loosely imprisoned in a cage of fine gold filigree—about her wrist.

'Noah,' she protested, 'I can't take this.'

'Not even if I told you that it would really hurt?' Then his mouth tightened. 'It's just a prop, Elizabeth. What you do with it...afterwards...is entirely up to you.'

Some prop, she thought. 'You must have it back,' she said, a little desperately. 'And the ring. Everything.'

'No. Thank you.' And for just a moment his eyes creased in a smile that rent her heart. 'They really wouldn't suit me.'

'I...I'll get my cloak,' she said, somewhat hoarsely. And as she bent to pick up the soft velvet cape the mirror assured her that pallor was no longer a problem. Her cheeks now had the sting of colour to them.

Downstairs the hotel lobby was overflowing with men in dinner jackets and women in glorious gowns, all apparently going to the open-air performance of *Aida*. But Noah didn't linger, despite several attempts to engage him in conversation. He swept her out to the waiting car and the driver immediately sped away.

'How far is it?' she asked as they reached the outskirts of the city, where the towering quarries that had supplied the stone for the pyramids formed a backdrop for an open-air market with a vast array of pots laid row upon row in the evening sun.

'You'll see the pyramids soon,' he promised. And he was right. Suddenly they were there, appearing as if by magic above the haze, much closer than she had expected. And, needing to touch something human, she reached for his hand.

'Oh, glory,' she murmured softly, and as if he understood he gently squeezed her fingers.

But they didn't stop, although she could see the stage set, the arena, and a few early arrivals, oddly out of place in their evening clothes, wandering around the vast necropolis. She turned questioningly to Noah.

'Just wait,' he said. The sun was lowering as the car finally pulled to a halt, and she realised that her hand was still held close in his. Noah climbed out and, holding out his arm to support her, led the way across the stony desert ground until they came to the edge of a ridge.

A little way below them, on the plains of Giza, stood the three great pyramids, surrounded by the ruins of much smaller tombs. The shadows had lengthened now, stretching endlessly as the sun sank slowly towards the desert, a huge ball of fire that seemed to blot out the sky. The sand blazed red for just a moment, and then it was over, and all that was left was a pink blush to colour the gathering purple where a single star winked brightly at her.

'That was incredible,' she said. 'Thank you.' The words didn't seem nearly enough, and it seemed for ever before he stirred and turned to her.

'An apology for what I said this afternoon seemed hardly sufficient,' he said a little stiffly. 'So, for what it's worth, that's it.'

Lizzie gasped. Noah Jordan did nothing by half measures. This afternoon he had cut her heart out with his tongue; now he had reduced her to tears with one stunning gesture. It just wasn't fair. She turned her head a little desperately, away from those intently searching eyes, back to the darkening pyramids. Anywhere so that he shouldn't see how vulnerable she was, that she was way out of her depth and had no idea which way the shore might be. Below her the floodlights had come on with the setting of the sun, and the crowds were beginning to arrive in ever-increasing numbers.

'A simple "I'm sorry" would have done, Noah. If you'd meant it. We'd better go, or we'll miss the start of the performance.' And she fled back to the car before he could see the tears glistening on her cheeks.

The performance was intensely moving—the story of the princess-slave and her love for an Egyptian soldier. It was a love to die for, and right now Lizzie knew just how that felt. She turned to Noah in the darkness. His profile, outlined by the lights reflected from the stage, was hard, unsmiling.

She was bitterly regretting her rejection of his apology, an overture that might have led to... what? She would never know. She had been too cautious—afraid of committing herself, afraid of being hurt beyond mending. And suddenly she knew that being hurt wasn't the worst thing that could happen to her. The worst thing was being afraid, not having the courage to risk her heart without the guarantee of a happy ending. Life carried no guarantees, as she well knew.

After the performance Noah took her to a small restaurant high in the citadel, far away from the opera crowd.

'I didn't expect you to go to quite this much trouble to honour our bet,' Lizzie said, trying to lighten the atmosphere as they were served a traditional *mezza* of hot and cold dishes.

'I couldn't have you telling Peter I don't keep my promises. This was the only performance I could find within the next six months.'

'I have no intention of seeing Peter in the foreseeable future.'

'You're going to have to face him,' he began, 'if Fran is—' He stopped as he saw her face involuntarily tighten at the mention of the other woman's name. 'Well, perhaps we should drop that particular subject before it spoils an excellent meal,' he suggested. 'Why don't you tell me what you thought of Domingo?'

But she did little talking. As they were served with a dish of succulent spiced lamb cooked with lemons and olives it was Noah who went out of his way to entertain her, with stories about the foibles of some of the great operatic divas. He was almost unbearably kind in his attempt to distract her, making her feel even more wretched that she had spurned his overture of peace.

And despite Lizzie's protestations that she could eat nothing more Noah instructed the waiter to bring *khoushaf*—a delicious fruit salad studded with pistachio nuts and pine kernels and flavoured with rose and orange flower water—so that she could at least taste it and finish her meal in a thoroughly Arab style.

She was half-asleep as they drove back to the hotel, and Noah put his arm around her and drew her against his shoulder. It was the most blissful agony. And he kept her hand in his as they strolled through the lobby.

Once inside their suite he opened her bedroom door before turning to her as if he wanted to say something.

'Yes?' Lizzie prompted as he seemed about to turn away.

He shook his head, but then, almost reluctantly, he said, 'Olivia was right about you, Elizabeth . . .'

'Right?' Lizzie was suddenly jolted wide awake. 'But I thought she told you—'

Noah wasn't interested in what she thought. 'Despite the fact that you are without doubt the most provoking, the most impertinent and downright reckless young woman I have ever met—'

'*I'm* provoking—' Her heated challenge was cut off as he brushed her cheek with the back of his fingers.

'Positively infuriating,' he continued softly. 'Despite all that, Elizabeth, you would be very easy to love.'

Her heart gave a little skip, a dance of delight, and she reached for him. 'Then ... love me,' she whispered, slipping her arms about his neck.

For a moment his lips hovered barely an inch from her own, and she could feel the warmth of his body as she pressed close. Then he took her hands away and stepped back. 'I guess I never was much good at taking second place.' And when she could bear to open her eyes she saw that his face was wearing its sardonic disguise. 'I'm glad you enjoyed the evening, Elizabeth. But, as you went to such pains to point out, a simple thank you is all that's necessary. I'll see you in the morning.'

Noah refused to let her go down to the cottage, insisting that he needed her in London as his hostess, although in truth they did little entertaining. But to the outside world he was certainly the model of the devoted husband, bringing her flowers every day and making strenuous efforts to amuse her.

It was almost unbearable. One evening she tried to make him rebel by suggesting that she would like to see a local showing of the Walt Disney version of *Beauty and the Beast*. He didn't bat an eyelid. It was only his somewhat wry enquiry as to whether she thought his likeness to the beast quite remarkable that just for a moment recalled the piquant discord that had so enlivened their early exchanges.

To the outside world it must have appeared the perfect marriage. But at night, when Lizzie curled up alone, the hollow reality of their mock marriage asserted itself.

In the morning Noah was always there when she woke, when Mrs Harper brought up tea and the newspapers—relaxed in his dressing-gown, propped against the bedhead, apparently amusing his new wife. He *was* both amusing and charming whenever there was anyone to be convinced. And when they were alone he was as distant as the far side of the moon. What to the world looked like perfection was only perfect hell.

Lizzie had no idea where Noah was sleeping—knew only that he was avoiding the vast four-poster bed. She assumed that he was taking himself to the top floor of the house, where there were a number of small, unused rooms that Mrs Harper rarely went into. Then one night a month or so later, after a particularly sultry day, thunder began to roll ominously.

Lizzie ran to the windows to try and shut it out, but the sound seemed to reverberate through her bones. She stood it as long as she could, expecting Noah to appear at any moment to make sure that she was all right. Then a clap almost directly overhead sent her running through the house, searching for human contact, flinging open the bedroom doors, calling his name.

He didn't answer. For the simple reason that he wasn't there. With a sudden flash of hope she flew down the stairs, expecting to find him stretched out on a sofa somewhere, or working late in the study, but the house was quite empty.

A sudden hammering at the front door made her jump out of her skin. Then she flew to it with relief. Noah had gone out somewhere and forgotten his key. It was only after she had drawn back the bolts and opened the door that she remembered that Noah would have come through the mews at the rear.

'Is everything all right, Mrs Jordan? We had a radio-call that your alarm has gone off at headquarters.' It was the guards from the security firm who monitored Noah's alarm system.

Desperately conscious that she was clad only in her childish pyjamas, Lizzie cringed. 'I'm sorry. I must have set it off when I came downstairs... The thunder... startled me.'

'Would you like us to look around? Make absolutely sure?'

'That won't be necessary.' Noah's voice was brisk, despite the fact that he had clearly been running. 'I'm sorry you've been called out on a false alarm.'

Reassured, the men finally departed, leaving Noah and Lizzie staring at one another in the entrance hall. 'You're wet,' she said finally. More than that—his jeans and black polo shirt were soaked and he was unshaven.

He wiped his hand across his face. 'It's raining,' he said. 'Why aren't you in bed?' He didn't wait for her answer but crossed into the drawing room and put a match to the fire already laid in the grate. His complete lack of emotion was too much.

'Noah, where were you?' Her voice broke on a sob. 'I was so scared... Idiotic... I just can't help it...' But before she could finish, tell him about her stupid fear of thunder, he was across the room and holding her, his arms a refuge, the rough bristle of his chin bliss against her cheek.

'You're shivering.' He made an impatient sound. 'I'm soaking you—making it worse.' He made a move to draw away, but she clung to him.

'No, I don't care,' she said quickly. 'Just hold me.' She laid her head against his chest. 'When I woke up and realised I was completely on my own...' She looked up into his face, her eyes huge as they demanded an answer to her unspoken question.

'Elizabeth, I'm sorry...'

He seemed unable to go on, and with chilling insight, an ominous sense of intuition that turned her face to the colour of ashes, she knew and tried to fling away from him. Peter had gone back to New York to pack up their apartment, but Fran had stayed behind to avoid the unnecessary risk of flying, and to sort out the details of the new home they had found with Noah's help.

Lizzie wrenched at her arms, but Noah held her fast. 'Listen to me.'

'No, don't tell me.' She didn't want to hear, and she began to beat at him and kick him and struggle as if her life depended on it.

'Stop this!' He shook her, but she kept on fighting, as if for her life. 'Listen to me—'

'I won't listen. You were with Fran,' she screamed at him, her hands flailing uselessly as he held her at arm's length. 'The nobility didn't take long to wear off. Not so much Galahad, it seems, as Lancelot...'

'You're upset; you don't know what you're saying—'

'Don't I? I think I do. You haven't been able to take your eyes off her. Even at the wedding it was there. Something.' She shook her head, her hair flying wildly. 'You were so *protective*. She mustn't be hurt by that nasty Lizzie French who couldn't be trusted with someone else's husband...I can't believe the sheer hypocrisy of it. The moment Peter left the country you couldn't wait to move in for the kill.'

Her eyes had darkened to indigo. 'How long did it take to seduce her, Noah?' she demanded. 'Did she fight every inch of the way for her honour before succumbing to the totally irresist—' her voice caught on a sob

'—irresistible charms of Noah Jordan?' Then with a groan of agony she collapsed to her knees, her wrists still held in his vice-like grip.

He dropped to his knees before her, refusing to let her go. 'Would it matter?' he demanded, his face too close to hers, rain dripping from his hair, running down his face, eyes like searchlights as he scoured her soul for the answer.

'Damn you, Noah. Do you have to have it all?' And she finally laid her head against his chest and sobbed. 'You know it matters.'

For a little while he was content to hold her, crooning softly into her hair, stroking her back. 'Tell me,' he insisted finally, when she was quieter. 'Tell me why it matters.'

Tell him? What could she tell him? Only the truth. Finally, irrevocably. She lifted her face to his. 'I love you, Noah Jordan. I want you so much that it's like a pain that won't go away.'

He said nothing for a while. 'How... how can you possibly love me? After what I've done to you?'

'It just happened—' Another little sob hiccuped through her. 'Some time between the fights.'

'In Cairo...was that what you were trying to tell me?'

'What else?'

'I thought... that you felt you had to. That I expected it after the silly way I'd behaved that morning...'

'You were teasing. I knew that the moment Mrs Harper knocked on the door. I was planning to avenge myself...' Some revenge, she thought drily. 'You never gave me the chance.'

There was a long silence. 'And Peter?' he asked finally.

Lizzie gave a little shake of her head. 'Peter and I have known one another a long time. Too long, perhaps. He hurt my pride a little, as I hurt his. But he couldn't break my heart—because once I'd met you, Noah, I discovered that it had never been his to break.'

He stared at her as if she were a newly discovered masterpiece. 'Oh, Lord, what a pair of fools we've been.' He raised his hand and very gently brushed away the tears from her cheeks. 'Elizabeth, I know we married each other for all the wrong reasons, that I promised you could leave after six months... But is it just possible that you would stay with me for the right ones—to have and to hold, in sickness and health, till death do us part?'

It was glorious and terrifying all at once, and although she opened her mouth she found she couldn't speak. 'Fran?' she finally whispered.

'Fran is my sister.'

'Your sister?' He placed a finger lightly on her lips as her eyes widened in shock.

'My half-sister, to be more accurate. My mother's child. I'll show you.' He stood up and, with his arm about her waist, took her across to the portrait that had attracted her attention the first evening that he had brought her to his house. 'That is my mother.'

And now she could see—the soft cloud of dark hair, that same ready smile. 'The likeness is... unmistakable. I can't think why I didn't see it before.' She turned to him. 'Olivia told me that she left...'

'She was a singer—a coloratura soprano. I saw her perform once. My father took me. A birthday treat. I thought she was a queen. She wasn't, of course. She wasn't a star, but with luck and the right breaks she might have made it. I'm afraid that losing her broke my father's heart, but it was always on the cards. She was so much younger than him.'

Lizzie turned to him. 'How much younger?'

'Twenty-five years. Oh, Lizzie,' he murmured, and her name suddenly had a tender new sound. His lips brushed her hair, her temples, her throat.

'And where have you been sleeping?' she asked a little desperately as things began to slip out of control.

'Lizzie, Lizzie, you ask so many questions...' And he cradled her face in his long fingers and kissed her, his mouth a gentle question of his own. A question that at last she was able to answer without reservation.

'Noah,' she whispered breathlessly a little while later, drawing back slightly.

He regarded her with eyes that smoked dangerously. 'What is it? Are you having second thoughts?'

'Second thoughts, third thoughts, fourth thoughts— all of them wonderful,' she said as she trailed the tip of her finger along his cheek-bone, down the line of his jaw until finally she traced the outline of his fiercely sensual mouth. 'I just thought that perhaps we should get out of these wet clothes.'

'Pleased to help, ma'am,' he murmured, but she caught his wrists as he began to undo the buttons of her pyjama top.

'I'd rather like to try the four-poster.'

'And I had the distinct impression that you enjoyed the floor—or perhaps you're getting a little old for such—?'

'Who's old?' she demanded.

'You are. Or had you forgotten it's your birthday today?'

'Today...?' She looked at the clock. It was ten minutes past midnight.

'My... Yes, I had!'

'I haven't.' He laughed softly and, picking her up, began to carry her up the curving staircase. 'And I can't wait to give you a very special present.'

* * *

'You still haven't told me where you've been sleeping,' Lizzie murmured sleepily, a long time later.

'I've been sleeping in the basement at the gallery. That's why I knew the alarm had gone off. They're linked.'

'The basement?' That bare, echoing cheerless place. 'Why?'

'Because I couldn't sleep alongside you and not make love to you.'

Lizzie remembered the morning after the wedding, how she had longed for him. 'I can sympathise with that,' she said. 'But there are dozens of rooms here—'

'I'm not made of wood, my love.'

'You could have fooled me.' She kissed him—just to see what it was like when she did it all by herself.

'That was...nice. Why don't you try it again?'

'Not so fast. Tell me, what happened to the cynic who didn't believe in love? I thought you didn't have a heart?'

'I haven't got a heart, Lizzie. I've given it to you.' Then he laughed out loud. 'You look positively smug, you little hussy.'

'Well, a girl likes to know that she's irresistible.'

'Believe it.' He moulded a breast in the palm of his hand, bending to taste her warm skin, the sweet, proud bud. Then slowly he drew back, and his hand traced the curve of her abdomen, his brows drawn together in the slightest frown.

'What is it?' Lizzie demanded.

He shook his head. 'I must be getting slow-witted in my old age. When were you going to tell me, or weren't you going to bother?'

Lizzie felt a slow flush rise to her cheeks. 'You said you could always tell... Do you mind?'

'Mind? That you are carrying my child? I think, my love, that I have to be the happiest man alive.'

* * *

'I still don't understand why you were so convinced that Fran was your sister,' Lizzie said over breakfast a long time later. 'Did you know that your mother had had another child?'

'No. And I don't suppose my father would have told me, even if he had known. But she married her American. At least, I assume they were married—I won't have all the details until Peter gets back. She was touring there when she fell in love with one of the musicians in the orchestra.'

'The Puccini factor?' she asked gently.

'Maybe. Opera is all passion...'

'Olivia told me that they were killed in a hurricane.'

'Yes. Dad came to school and told me that she was dead. And then at your father's wedding suddenly there was Fran. It was like a step back into the past. Or being confronted by a ghost. Impossible, and yet just possible. I followed her when she left the marquee, meaning to speak to her, find out who she was. Instead I ran into that gruesome little scene between the three of you.'

Lizzie remembered that all too clearly. 'And she told you that her mother had been a singer.'

'You can see that I had to find out. That's why I invited them to the opera.' He looked uncomfortable. 'And I'd seen Peter's reaction to you, your shock at the news. It was obvious there was something between the two of you. It was weird. I just wanted to protect her, help her. I felt so... fierce about her. And you appeared to offer some kind of threat. Olivia was very convincing about your lack of scruples—'

'Did Fran know who you were?'

'She hadn't a clue. Still hasn't...but I finally told Peter my suspicions.'

'That's what you wanted to talk to him about at the wedding party,' Lizzie breathed.

'Yes. I'd flown to New York myself, but I'd had so little time and not nearly enough information. Fran was adopted when... when her parents were killed, and had taken her adoptive parents' name, so I needed him to check some details—things he could find out without raising her suspicions. I had a letter from him a couple of days ago, with a copy of Fran's birth certificate. There's no doubt about it.'

'When are you going to tell her?'

'Not yet. I thought we'd wait until Peter gets back. I think he should be the one to tell her. And I'll have to tell Olivia. Perhaps we could have a family party here? There are some things of my mother's that I think she should have... Perhaps even that portrait.'

'Of course.' She reached across and covered his hand. 'It will be lovely.'

He gazed across at her. 'Quite lovely. And, talking of parties, it's time you had your birthday present.'

'I thought I'd already had that,' she said. And she giggled as he took her across to the study.

'I think, sweet hussy, that you might lose count of the birthdays that are in store for you...' And there was a considerable pause before he lifted a large, rectangular-shaped parcel wrapped in heavy brown paper onto the desk.

'It looks like a painting,' she said, undoing the string.

'It is a painting.'

She looked up at him sternly. 'Now you've spoiled the surprise...' But as she threw back the paper she let out a squeal of delight. 'Noah, it's my pig—my lovely, fat pig. But it was auctioned last week for absolutely thousands...'

'Thousands that you immediately donated to the village minibus appeal.'

She waved that aside as totally unimportant. 'You were sitting beside me. How on earth did you manage it?'

He raised his shoulders in a self-deprecating little shrug. 'I have very speaking eyebrows. Are you pleased?' he asked, propping himself on the desk.

'Would you like me to show you how pleased?' she offered, wrapping her arms about his neck.

There was a small cough from behind them. 'I think we'd better interrupt before this goes any further.'

Lizzie swung around. 'Olivia—Daddy!'

'Happy birthday, darling.' Her father pressed a small box into her hand. 'A little present for you.' He nodded towards the painting on the desk. 'Where on earth are you going to hang that?' he asked, looking around at the work of the great modern artists displayed upon the walls.

'In the morning room...'

'At the cottage...'

Lizzie and Noah declared at the same moment. They glared at one another for a second and then burst out laughing. 'We'll find somewhere for it,' Noah promised, and turned back to Olivia. 'Will you join us for a celebration this evening?'

'I think we'd be *de trop*, darling,' she said.

'And we're only just recovering from last night. Did you see the awards?' James asked.

'Awards?'

James produced a video from his pocket. 'You might be interested in seeing this, Lizzie.' He slotted it into the machine in the corner of the room and pressed the start button. They all watched as a distinguished knighted actor read out a list of nominations for actress of the year, one of whom was Olivia.

The clips began to roll and suddenly there was Olivia in close-up, her knuckles white as she gripped a telephone.

'We're saved, darling. I've got the man in the palm of my hand. Lord, but it took some acting to convince the old fool...but it's the perfect cover...' There was a pause while she listened and then Olivia began to laugh softly. 'I can't run away from my honeymoon, my darling, much as I'd like to. But after that, well... I'm keeping my London flat so I can see you any time I want. The only fly in the ointment is Daddy's little girl...she's so protective...but I'm working on a little plan to deal with her...'

'And the winner is...Olivia Jordan for her thrilling portrayal of—' James leaned forward and switched it off.

'But they haven't seen my touching acceptance speech,' Olivia complained.

'Another time, darling,' James murmured. His eyes offered Lizzie an apology, and the room became totally silent as three pairs of eyes turned on Olivia.

'What is it? What's the matter?' She gave an awkward little laugh. 'I know what this is. You think I stole my master plan from my latest role... Well, what if I did? I was watching the print sent by the studio and I thought...' She raised a defiant little chin. 'What's so funny?' she demanded as James and Noah and Lizzie began to laugh. 'It worked, didn't it?'

'Yes,' Lizzie gasped, clinging helplessly to Noah, tears of laughter running down her cheeks. 'In fact, I honestly believe you should have an Oscar.'

This March, Harlequin brings you
a wonderful collection of
stories celebrating family, in...

YOURS, MINE & Ours

Written by three of your favorite authors

PENNY JORDAN
CATHY GILLEN THACKER
MARISA CARROLL

How do two families become one? Just add love!
Available anywhere Harlequin books are sold.

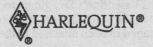

HARLEQUIN®

Look us up on-line at: http://www.romance.net

HREQ397

HARLEQUIN®

Don't miss these Harlequin favorites by some of our most
distinguished authors!
And now, you can receive a discount by ordering two or more titles!

HT#25645	THREE GROOMS AND A WIFE by JoAnn Ross	$3.25 U.S. $3.75 CAN.	☐ ☐
HT#25647	NOT THIS GUY by Glenda Sanders	$3.25 U.S. $3.75 CAN.	☐ ☐
HP#11725	THE WRONG KIND OF WIFE by Roberta Leigh	$3.25 U.S. $3.75 CAN.	☐ ☐
HP#11755	TIGER EYES by Robyn Donald	$3.25 U.S. $3.75 CAN.	☐ ☐
HR#03416	A WIFE IN WAITING by Jessica Steele	$3.25 U.S. $3.75 CAN.	☐ ☐
HR#03419	KIT AND THE COWBOY by Rebecca Winters	$3.25 U.S. $3.75 CAN.	☐ ☐
HS#70622	KIM & THE COWBOY by Margot Dalton	$3.50 U.S. $3.99 CAN.	☐ ☐
HS#70642	MONDAY'S CHILD by Janice Kaiser	$3.75 U.S. $4.25 CAN.	☐ ☐
HI#22342	BABY VS. THE BAR by M.J. Rodgers	$3.50 U.S. $3.99 CAN.	☐ ☐
HI#22382	SEE ME IN YOUR DREAMS by Patricia Rosemoor	$3.75 U.S. $4.25 CAN.	☐ ☐
HAR#16538	KISSED BY THE SEA by Rebecca Flanders	$3.50 U.S. $3.99 CAN.	☐ ☐
HAR#16603	MOMMY ON BOARD by Muriel Jensen	$3.50 U.S. $3.99 CAN.	☐ ☐
HH#28885	DESERT ROGUE by Erine Yorke	$4.50 U.S. $4.99 CAN.	☐ ☐
HH#28911	THE NORMAN'S HEART by Margaret Moore	$4.50 U.S. $4.99 CAN.	☐ ☐

(limited quantities available on certain titles)

	AMOUNT	$
DEDUCT:	10% DISCOUNT FOR 2+ BOOKS	$
ADD:	POSTAGE & HANDLING	$
	($1.00 for one book, 50¢ for each additional)	
	APPLICABLE TAXES*	$_____
	TOTAL PAYABLE	$_____
	(check or money order—please do not send cash)	

To order, complete this form and send it, along with a check or money order for the
total above, payable to Harlequin Books, to: **In the U.S.:** 3010 Walden Avenue,
P.O. Box 9047, Buffalo, NY 14269-9047; **In Canada:** P.O. Box 613, Fort Erie, Ontario,
L2A 5X3.

Name:_____

Address: _____ City: _____

State/Prov.: _____ Zip/Postal Code:_____

*New York residents remit applicable sales taxes.
 Canadian residents remit applicable GST and provincial taxes.
Look us up on-line at: http://www.romance.net

HBACK-JM4

HARLEQUIN PRESENTS®

HARLEQUIN PRESENTS
men you won't be able to resist falling in love with...

HARLEQUIN PRESENTS
women who have feelings just like your own...

HARLEQUIN PRESENTS
powerful passion in exotic international settings...

HARLEQUIN PRESENTS
intense, dramatic stories that will keep you turning
to the very last page...

HARLEQUIN PRESENTS
The world's bestselling romance series!